A Bone-Chilling Dis...

Lila spurred her horse in [...]
something a lot more chilli[...]
imagined finding on Skull M[...]

"Holy cow!" Ned whispe[...] up on his reins
and staring. "Are those *human* skeletons?"

"I'm afraid so."

Lila dismounted and, with her Winchester still
clenched tightly in her fist, she went to the four broken
and chewed-up skeletons. She wouldn't have known for
certain that there were four if it hadn't been for the skulls,
because the body bones had been scattered over what had
once been a prospector's camp.

"What do you think happened!" Ned cried. "Did that
grizzly kill and then eat them all?"

"Not unless she was carrying a rifle," Lila replied, her
voice quiet and low. "Because what I'm seeing are bullet holes in the skulls."

DON'T MISS THESE
ALL-ACTION WESTERN SERIES
FROM THE BERKLEY PUBLISHING GROUP

THE GUNSMITH by J. R. Roberts
Clint Adams was a legend among lawmen, outlaws, and ladies. They called him . . . the Gunsmith.

LONGARM by Tabor Evans
The popular long-running series about Deputy U.S. Marshal Custis Long—his life, his loves, his fight for justice.

SLOCUM by Jake Logan
Today's longest-running action Western. John Slocum rides a deadly trail of hot blood and cold steel.

BUSHWHACKERS by B. J. Lanagan
An action-packed series by the creators of Longarm! The rousing adventures of the most brutal gang of cutthroats ever assembled—Quantrill's Raiders.

DIAMONDBACK by Guy Brewer
Dex Yancey is Diamondback, a Southern gentleman turned con man when his brother cheats him out of the family fortune. Ladies love him. Gamblers hate him. But nobody pulls one over on Dex . . .

WILDGUN by Jack Hanson
The blazing adventures of mountain man Will Barlow—from the creators of Longarm!

TEXAS TRACKER by Tom Calhoun
J.T. Law: the most relentless—and dangerous—manhunter in all Texas. Where sheriffs and posses fail, he's the best man to bring in the most vicious outlaws—for a price.

TABOR EVANS

LONGARM

AND THE SKULL
MOUNTAIN GOLD

JOVE BOOKS, NEW YORK

THE BERKLEY PUBLISHING GROUP
Published by the Penguin Group
Penguin Group (USA) Inc.
375 Hudson Street, New York, New York 10014, USA
Penguin Group (Canada), 90 Eglinton Avenue East, Suite 700, Toronto, Ontario M4P 2Y3, Canada
(a division of Pearson Penguin Canada Inc.)
Penguin Books Ltd., 80 Strand, London WC2R 0RL, England
Penguin Group Ireland, 25 St. Stephen's Green, Dublin 2, Ireland (a division of Penguin Books Ltd.)
Penguin Group (Australia), 250 Camberwell Road, Camberwell, Victoria 3124, Australia
(a division of Pearson Australia Group Pty. Ltd.)
Penguin Books India Pvt. Ltd., 11 Community Centre, Panchsheel Park, New Delhi—110 017, India
Penguin Group (NZ), 67 Apollo Drive, Rosedale, North Shore 0632, New Zealand
(a division of Pearson New Zealand Ltd.)
Penguin Books (South Africa) (Pty.) Ltd., 24 Sturdee Avenue, Rosebank, Johannesburg 2196,
South Africa

Penguin Books Ltd., Registered Offices: 80 Strand, London WC2R 0RL, England

This is a work of fiction. Names, characters, places, and incidents either are the product of the author's imagination or are used fictitiously, and any resemblance to actual persons, living or dead, business establishments, events, or locales is entirely coincidental.

LONGARM AND THE SKULL MOUNTAIN GOLD

A Jove Book / published by arrangement with the author

PRINTING HISTORY
Jove edition / February 2010

Copyright © 2010 by Penguin Group (USA) Inc.
Cover illustration by Miro Sinovcic.

ISBN: 978-0-515-14757-5

JOVE®
Jove Books are published by The Berkley Publishing Group,
a division of Penguin Group (USA) Inc.,
375 Hudson Street, New York, New York 10014.
JOVE® is a registered trademark of Penguin Group (USA) Inc.
The "J" design is a trademark of Penguin Group (USA) Inc.

PRINTED IN THE UNITED STATES OF AMERICA

10 9 8 7 6 5 4 3 2 1

Chapter 1

Longarm was feeling poor, mighty damn poor. He'd been a United States Deputy Marshal for many years, but he never seemed to be able to get ahead financially. Where did all of his money go after each paycheck? Well, for one thing, he was sending money to a destitute widow in Wyoming who had lost her husband in a stagecoach holdup. The woman had four little kids and a slew of bills that had mounted up while trying to save her husband's life. The wounded man had eventually died, and now his widow was faced with losing her homestead and every other thing that she and her deceased husband had ever owned. On top of that there were a couple of other people that Longarm regularly sent a few dollars to, including a Navajo boy in Arizona who had broken his back chasing mustangs and was now partially paralyzed. The boy had helped Longarm track a vicious killer across his huge reservation and had risked his life to save Longarm's skin. Now the kid needed money for an operation by a renowned Philadelphia surgeon or else he'd never walk again. Longarm just couldn't bear the idea of the kid never walking again. And then there were Longarm's own needs, which, although he was a bachelor, seemed considerable because he had a few expensive tastes. He insisted on good food, stayed away from bad liquor, and loved to entertain an unending flow of beautiful and willing women.

So that Monday morning, as he climbed the steps of the U.S. Marshal's office near the Denver Mint, Longarm was determined to have a showdown with his friend and his boss, Marshal Billy Vail. He would demand a raise, which he had not received in over three years. He'd explain to Billy that he simply had to make more money . . . or else find another line of work. After all, he wasn't getting any younger, and given the risks he took in his job, he deserved to be paid double the sixty dollars a month he was currently receiving. And he'd even talked to the local sheriff, who had offered him a job starting at seventy-five dollars a month. Hell, Longarm thought, the Denver sheriff knows I'm worth every penny of that and more.

"I'd like to see Billy this morning," Longarm told the man's new secretary, a middle-aged woman who looked owlish in her thick glasses.

"Is Marshal Vail expecting *you* this morning?" the woman demanded in a way that Longarm didn't care for in the least.

Longarm frowned and glared at the woman in his most menacing fashion. This was a new secretary and she didn't seem to understand that he was the best United States Marshal in the building, and when he wanted to see the boss, he sure didn't have to make any damned appointment.

"Ma'am, Billy and I go back a long, long ways, and I can go in to see him any time that I want."

"He's seeing someone else right now," the woman announced. "And I don't think he wants to be interrupted."

"Well," Longarm said, stepping around the woman's desk and heading for Billy Vail's private office, "I don't care if he's seeing the president of the United States right now."

"Wait, please!"

But Longarm was in no mood to wait, so he barged into Billy's office and skidded to a stop on the polished hardwood floor. Billy held a pretty young woman in his arms and she definitely was not his devoted wife and the mother of his children.

"Oh," Longarm said, shocked and at a loss for words. "I didn't know you were . . ."

"This is not what it appears to be," Billy said, still holding the beautiful woman.

"Glad to hear that," Longarm said, backing toward the doorway. "I'll come back later."

"Sit down," Billy ordered. "Miss Chandler was just about to leave."

"Not on my account, I hope."

The woman took a silk handkerchief from her purse and wiped her eyes, which were red from prolonged crying. Longarm felt awful for his rude intrusion and he apologized. "Miss, I'm sorry to have interrupted you and Billy. I mean, Marshal Vail."

"It's all right," she said, managing a smile.

Longarm couldn't help but notice that she was probably about twenty-five, stood about five feet ten inches, and was stunning. She had a heart-shaped face, blue eyes, and blonde hair. Her figure, from what he could tell, was voluptuous. She wore a turquoise and silver bracelet with matching earrings, but no wedding ring.

"Miss Chandler, this is my finest deputy marshal, Custis Long."

Longarm removed his snuff-brown Stetson and offered the lady a slight bow. He was, after all, a gentleman, a man born and raised well in West Virginia, and one who had been taught to respect all women, even whores, unless they proved to be so uncouth as to be unworthy of his respect.

"Pleased to meet you, Miss Chandler."

Billy released the woman, who then took Longarm's hand in her own and said, "Likewise, I'm sure."

Billy said, "Miss Lila Chandler is from around Grants, New Mexico, where her family has a small cattle ranch. Longarm, you may remember her father, the legendary Marshal Kenyon Chandler."

A light turned on in Longarm's head and he replied, "I certainly do. Kenyon Chandler was the federal marshal who single-handedly tracked down the Brody Gang and killed all three brothers in a Santa Fe saloon shootout about ten years ago."

The young woman lifted her chin proudly. "Yes, that's my father. He was shot three times in that fight but still managed to come out of that saloon standing. I'm proud to say that the Brody brothers went out feet first and our territory was rid of some of the worst and most vicious white men in its storied history."

"Is your father still a United States Marshal?"

"That's the discussion we were just having when you busted in here without any announcement," Billy said. "I was just telling Miss Lila Chandler how much we respect her father and wish him the best in his retirement."

"But he doesn't *want* to retire!" Lila cried out. "My poor father can't afford to retire because both he and Mother are sick and need medical care. My parents are destitute! *Destitute*, Marshal Vail! We all know that my father has given his life to upholding the law in New Mexico Territory. He's been shot, stabbed, and beaten, and now put out to pasture where there isn't a blade of grass to eat. Please, Marshal Vail, the long and dangerous years my dear father served this country ought to be worth some kind of reward. Some kind of just payment now in his time of greatest need."

"I'm sorry about your father," Billy said, looking upset and deeply moved by the woman's pleas. "I really am. Marshal Kenyon Chandler is an American hero. There has never been a finer U.S. Marshal. But what can I do?"

"Petition the United States Congress or the president or someone to help my father. After all his years of duty and service to our country, a federal pension of only eleven dollars a month is an insult!"

"*Eleven* dollars?" Longarm blurted. "Is that all Marshal Chandler is going to receive?"

"That's right. Why, given the many lingering injuries he suffered in the line of duty, that doesn't even pay his doctor bills, much less his other expenses. We've sold our cattle and horses. We've mortgaged our ranch to the hilt, and now we're going to lose it if something can't be done."

Lila turned away for a moment, overcome with emotion.

Longarm turned to Billy. "Marshal Chandler only gets *eleven* dollars a month?"

Billy couldn't meet his eyes and walked slowly around behind his desk, finally taking a seat and then running his hand across his face. "Custis, I know that is a pittance, but the United States Congress is long overdue in raising the pensions of its long-faithful and retired law officers. There has been talk of doubling the pension and even adding some extra for those that have suffered permanent injuries due to their service to this country . . . but the money has so far not been authorized."

"Then see if you can help get it authorized!" Lila Chandler pleaded. "My father is in failing health. He carries a bullet in his side that is slowly working its way deeper toward his heart! He can't afford surgery to have that bullet removed and now he can't even afford to help Mother survive."

"It's a travesty," Longarm growled. "An insult."

"Of course it is," Lila said. "And you'll be treated the same some day when you're old and suffering like my father from all the injuries you've received in the line of duty."

"I'll write my superiors in Washington, D.C.," Billy vowed, fists clenched. "I'll tell them that Marshal Kenyon Chandler is a hero out in the West and they simply have to find money to help him in his time of need."

Miss Chandler nodded. "Thank you so much, Marshal Vail. *When* will you write this letter?"

"Today! I'll write it today and put it in the strongest words possible," Billy promised.

She smiled. "That's wonderful news. How soon would this letter be read by your superiors in Washington, D.C.?"

"In a week or ten days."

"And then may I ask what most likely will happen?"

"I really don't know," Billy admitted. "But if I don't hear something positive in your father's desperate case, then I'll send a telegram directly to the president of these United States."

"Thank you so much! My father told me that you would do your very best to try and help him and my mother."

"I can't promise you or your father anything, Miss Chandler. I'm just a public servant and my voice is a long way from Washington and the powers that be. But I give you my solemn word of honor that I will not let this matter of your father and his pitiful pension slip from my mind for a single moment. We will get some help for him or . . ."

"Or what?" Longarm asked, knowing that his boss had no influence in the nation's capitol.

"Or I'll use my own vacation time and take a train to Washington where I'll personally present myself and plead for financial help for Marshal Kenyon Chandler."

Lila Chandler wiped her eyes dry and said, "Marshal Vail, my father always said you were a fine and honest man. He said that you'd do your very best to help him out. And now that I've met with you and spoken of my father's sad situation, I'm sure that he was right about you."

"I'm touched and honored," Billy said, rising from his desk chair. "Where are you staying right now in Denver?"

"At the Belleview Hotel. I've got a return train ticket for this coming Saturday and I know that my parents are praying for your help and support. I would send them an immediate telegram except that . . ."

"That what?" Longarm asked.

"I'm very short of funds," she admitted. "But that's neither here nor there. As long as my father gets some help, then I'll go to any sacrifice."

"They will have help, and soon," Billy promised.

Miss Lila Chandler seemed too overcome to reply, so she turned and left the office.

"Custis, please close my door and have a chair," Billy said, sounding subdued after the young woman had departed.

Longarm closed the door, his mind on the woman and what she had just told them. "Well, Billy, what do you think will happen in response to your Washington, D.C., letter?"

"I'm afraid that absolutely nothing will happen," Billy replied, pacing back and forth in front of his up-stairs office window. "The government is in terrible financial shape and they are actually talking about *cutting* the salaries of federal officers, past and present."

"Cutting!" Longarm shouted, anger surging through his veins. "Billy, we are hardly earning a living wage right now! And hearing that a legend like Kenyon Chandler is only receiving a lousy eleven bucks a month in retirement pay is unbelievable."

"It's true," Billy said. "I had my secretary check. That's what Chandler is receiving and there are no pension raises in sight. Perhaps even a cut in pensions."

"That's an outrage," Longarm said hotly. "Out in the field we risk our lives while back in Washington the only thing they risk is indigestion from too much rich food and hangovers from too much fine French wine and caviar."

Billy managed a thin smile. "Nobody said life was fair, Custis. And when you hired on to be a federal officer of the law, you knew what the job paid."

"Yeah, sure. But I always thought that we'd have some kind of a decent retirement . . . if we survived."

"Well, now you know better," Billy said. He threw up his hands. "What else can I say? It's a thankless career that offers lousy pay and almost no retirement pension. We'll both get to keep our badges and be presented with a letter of commendation framed in a plaque suitable for our cottage walls."

Longarm scowled and went to the window to look

down on the street. Suddenly, the day didn't seem so sunny or the sky so blue. He watched Miss Chandler exit the federal building and head up Colfax Avenue, her head down and her lovely body slumped at the shoulders. "You know something, Boss?"

"What?"

"I don't think she really expects your letter to do anything for her father," Longarm mused aloud.

"Regrettably, Miss Chandler is probably correct."

"It's a travesty that a man as famous and respected as Kenyon Chandler is going to wind up destitute and lose that little New Mexico cattle ranch."

"Yes, it is. And from what the young woman told me earlier, it really isn't much of a cattle ranch. Just a couple hundred acres of sagebrush and grass."

"It's their home and they're losing it," Longarm said quietly as he turned to face his boss and friend. "And when I retire, I'll have nothing either. Unless, that is, I take a desk job and become a well-paid bureaucrat like you."

Billy's head jerked up and his eyes sparked with sudden anger. He was an average-size man and he'd been a fine lawman before he'd had to take a promotion to earn more money for his large family. Since being out of the field he'd gotten pale and flabby. Longarm didn't want to wind up in the same situation or physical condition as his boss, pushing papers around a shiny desktop in order to make more money.

"I make no apologies to you or anyone else, Custis. I have a wife and children to support, and a man does what he has to do to take care of his family. If he doesn't, he's not much of a man."

"I know. I'm sorry, Billy. That was a lousy remark and I apologize. But the reason I came up here to talk to you this morning was to ask for a substantial raise in pay."

"Not even remotely possible."

"I can see that now," Longarm said. "And I can see what will happen to me when I get old like Marshal Chandler. I'll wind up living hand to mouth, poor as a church mouse, and no one will care that I spent thirty years getting hurt to uphold my oath of office."

"I'm sure that by the time you decide to retire," Billy argued, "the federal government will have a much more generous retirement."

"I'm not sure of that at all," Longarm told the man, unable to hide an edge of bitterness in his voice.

"Custis, you need to start saving money instead of spending more than you earn," Billy told him. "Your tastes are too damned expensive and you're a sucker for every sob story you hear. How much money are you still sending to that Navajo boy every month?"

"Not all that much," Longarm replied.

"And that widow woman in Wyoming? Miss Heatherford? How about her?"

"I send a few dollars every month. For gawd sakes, Billy, the woman is losing everything!"

"I know," Billy said, shaking his head. "Every now and then I send her a few dollars as well."

"I didn't know that."

"There's a lot you don't know about me, Custis. I'm not as hard-hearted as you might think, and I have my own financial struggles."

"You make double my monthly salary."

"And earn every dime of it sitting here in this office every day listening to everyone bitch and complain. On top of that, I get an unending flow of stupid letters from Washington, D.C., from people telling me how to do my job when they've never even been out in the West!"

Longarm threw up his hands. "Take it easy, Billy. Just calm down. We're old friends, remember?"

"I remember, but . . . but when I hear a sad case like just now concerning former Marshal Kenyon Candler, a man that I *always* looked up to and respected, well, it really grates on me hard."

Longarm nodded with understanding. "How about we both chip in a few dollars for Miss Chandler to take back to New Mexico? Maybe pass the hat around the office and pay her train fare and hotel room costs?"

"That's a fine idea," Billy said, brightening. "In fact, that's an *excellent* idea! Will you do that this morning?"

"Why me?"

"Because everyone respects you and some even fear you enough so that they'll have to toss money into your hat."

"Okay," Longarm said, not looking forward to the necessary task. "But I hate to ask people to chip in money."

"Everyone hates to do that," Billy said, turning to a pile of paperwork. "But someone has to do it, and I'm assigning you the worthy task."

"All right," Longarm said, taking off his hat and turning it upside down in front of Billy. "You're first, Boss."

Billy chuckled, then removed his wallet and took out five dollars to toss in. "That ought to set the standard and get the ball rolling. Don't let anyone toss just coins. A dollar minimum, or you tell them I'll hear about it and remember how cheap they were come their next promotion time."

"That will help," Longarm said, turning to leave.

"Oh," Billy said. "What else besides the ridiculous idea of a pay raise was so important this morning that you barged past my new secretary?"

Longarm paused and gave the question a moment of thought. After what he'd just seen and heard, it would be pointless to demand a raise in pay. "Nothing," he said on his way out. "Nothing at all."

"There must have been something else important on your mind," Billy persisted. "Shoot."

"Some other time," Longarm told his boss.

"Tell me how much money you collect from my office for old Kenyon Chandler."

"I will."

"And bring it to me and I'll take it to the young lady at the Belleview Hotel before she gets back on that train bound for New Mexico."

"I'll take it to her, if you don't mind."

Billy blinked and then shook his head. "I don't think you ought to do that, Custis."

"Why not?"

"Because Miss Lila Chandler has enough troubles already without adding *you* to her list."

Longarm barked a laugh and pretended to look insulted. "Why, Boss, that's a hell of a hard thing to say!"

"Yeah, but true. You leave that young New Mexico lady alone, Custis. And that's an official order."

"I'll just deliver the office's donations that I collect this morning and extend her my heartfelt sympathy," he said.

"As long as that's *all* you extend to her," Billy said cryptically as he dug into his detestable stack of government paperwork.

Chapter 2

The Belleview Hotel had once held a gala opening with a great deal of fanfare. Then Governor Orvis Goldfield and his fat wife Irma had stayed at the hotel for a week and, if history recorded it correctly, neither had been sober during their entire stay. "Wild Bill" Hickok, as well as many other notables, had also stayed at the Belleview in its early glory days. But about five years ago the original owner, a wealthy silver mine operator, had died of food poisoning in his own hotel and his children had sold the establishment to a man named Max Hennefield, who had viewed the fine brick hotel as nothing more than a moneymaker. Hennefield had fired a competent staff and replaced it with incompetent people who were willing to work long hours for little pay. The room service was now nonexistent, the food now over-priced, and the liquor that was poured in the once-renowned saloon was now watered down.

Once the favored hotel of the rich and near rich, now the

Belleview Hotel was frequented by shady gamblers, lower level government employees, higher class whores, and traveling salesmen. The hotel rooms had been allowed to deteriorate to the point that the carpets were threadbare, the sheets were rarely changed, and you didn't frequent the hallways at night unless you were looking for quick, sordid love or trouble. In short, it wasn't a place that Longarm thought a proper ranch-raised young lady like Miss Lila Chandler should have been staying while visiting Denver on behalf of her nearly destitute parents. And yet, it was the place where Longarm sometimes took a woman after he had wined and dinned her and then sought the comfort of her flesh for an hour or maybe even two.

"Ahh," said the desk clerk, a greasy-haired man in his early fifties with bad teeth, who lit up with a sly smile. "How good to see you again! Only been a week since your last hourly stay with us."

"Two weeks is closer to it," Longarm corrected.

"And where," the desk clerk asked, "is your lady for tonight?"

"I didn't bring one."

The clerk raised his eyebrows in question, the unctuous smile still frozen on his long horse face. "Then perhaps you've come to meet a fair lady that is already upstairs?"

Longarm didn't appreciate the man's phony smile or his overt familiarity. The word was out that this hotel clerk was a petty thief and that he preferred the company of boys to that of women. "If I remember correctly, your name is Delbert. Isn't that right?"

"Yes, sir. Pleased that you'd remember. Now, which room would you like for the next few hours?"

"None of 'em. I'm here seeking one of your respectable female guests."

"Of course you are. Would you prefer Lulu or Molly for a short time? Both are available right now in rooms—"

"I'm not interested in either of them," Longarm snapped. "I came to visit a Miss Lila Chandler."

"Ah-ha! So, you're going for the jackpot tonight. Excellent choice!" The man rubbed his bony hands together and grinned, leaning over the counter. "I wish I could be in your place, because that woman is absolutely—"

Longarm reached across the counter, grabbed the clerk's dirty shirtfront, and hissed, "Shut up, Delbert, or I'll slam my fist so far down your throat that I'll be able to pull your guts up through your rotting teeth!"

Delbert struggled like a mouse caught in the jaws of a cat. "Please, don't hurt me! I was only complimenting you on your fine taste."

Longarm flung the desk clerk backward in disgust. "What room is the lady in, you little shit?"

"Room one-oh-four, just down the hallway to the right." Delbert smoothed out his food-stained shirtfront and backed well out of Longarm's reach. "I really don't appreciate being handled like that, Marshal Long. And I just might speak to your boss."

"Do that and I'll kick your butt all the way up through your nostrils."

"My, my," Delbert said, visibly growing pale. "We're very, very touchy tonight, aren't we, Custis?"

"Marshal Long."

"Marshal Long, or whatever," the clerk said dismissively. "Now, if you'll excuse me, I have work to do."

It was all that Longarm could do not to walk around the counter and then grab and throttle Delbert. Instead, he headed down the hallway and stopped at Miss Chandler's door to knock.

There was no answer. Longarm knocked louder and waited, but still no answer. "Damn," he muttered.

He supposed that the woman from northern New Mexico was already out to dinner. That was disappointing because he'd been hoping to treat her to a fine meal at a good steakhouse not more than two blocks from this hotel before giving her an office envelope containing over fifty much-needed dollars. Now he was momentarily at a loss as to what to do. He definitely did not want to give Delbert the envelope with the donations he'd gotten from his office. Delbert, the sneak thief, would no doubt skim from the office money or even dare to steal it and swear that it had been lifted by a guest while he'd turned his back on the envelope.

"Nope," Longarm said, as he headed back to the lobby, "I can't leave the money with that sly weasel."

"Looks like your romantic scheme for this evening is already off to a bad start," Delbert chirped from behind the safety of the registration desk. "How very, very sad!"

"Where did Miss Chandler go?"

Delbert shrugged his narrow shoulders and gave

Longarm that sickening grin again. "Who knows? Judging by her looks and manners, I'd say Miss Chandler is probably out to dinner with a *real* gentleman."

Longarm took one step toward the desk clerk and that was all that was needed to make the man whirl and disappear behind a curtain leading to a back office.

"Weasel!" Longarm shouted.

"Big, overgrown bully!" Delbert cried shrilly from behind the curtain.

Longarm stomped over to the hotel's combination saloon and dining room on the slim hope that Miss Chandler might be there eating alone.

And she *was* seated in the dining room, only she was in the company of a man old enough to be her father. Longarm didn't recognize him, but he was short, balding, and well dressed. A successful traveling salesman, Longarm thought, or a prosperous businessman, an out-of-town visitor who had been fooled by the Belleview's handsome exterior into assuming this was still a first-class hotel.

Longarm started to turn and leave, but Lila saw him in the doorway and jumped up. "Why, Marshal Long! What a pleasant surprise. Please, come and join us for supper."

Longarm didn't want to join *them* for supper. He wanted to take Miss Chandler to supper and enjoy her company all by himself.

"Ahh, maybe next time," Longarm hedged.

"No, please!" Lila insisted, hurrying over to take his hand and give it a tug. "My dining partner is Mr. Smith from St. Louis. The gentleman has kindly invited me to join him for a lovely supper and I know he would be most happy to also have you, a real Western lawman, as his guest."

"I doubt that," Longarm said, noting Smith's unfriendly gaze.

Lila leaned close and whispered, "I haven't had the money to eat anything worth calf slobber since I arrived, and Mr. Smith is more than willing to buy me the best this hotel dining room has to offer. And he'll do the same for you, so just smile, be charming, and enjoy a *free* meal."

"The food here is not that great."

"It will still be free, won't it? And Mr. Smith is buying the best whiskey and wine that this hotel stocks. And besides, he's already getting drunk and a little too forward for my taste. I need a real gentleman at my side."

"Well," Longarm hedged, "in that case, I guess I will join you at the table."

"That would be a smart move. Mr. Smith is primed and loaded."

"He's not going to be happy with me joining you at his table," Longarm told her. "Mr. Smith is no doubt an alias and the man is probably married and hoping to get lucky tonight with a young beauty like yourself."

"Shhh!" Lila took his arm and dragged him over to their table. "Mr. Smith, I'd like you to meet Marshal Custis Long."

Smith tried to smile but failed, and took a deep drink from his glass of whiskey. He made a face as if the whiskey were sour.

Pulling over a chair from another table, Longarm said, "Miss Chandler tells me that you are from St. Louis. What brings you to our fair city of Denver?"

"Business."

"What kind of business?"

Smith sighed, as if answering the question would be an effort. "I'm in the cattle business. I sell grain and medicines, branding irons, and various other necessities related to the Western cattle industry."

"Well, isn't that interesting," Lila said brightly. "Mr. Smith is here alone this week and is hoping to close a big deal with one of Denver's main cattle feeding lots."

"Is that right?" Longarm said, trying to sound interested.

"That's right," Smith replied. "But I'm sure that what you do is far more interesting."

"Sometimes," Longarm agreed.

"Have you ever had to use that big six-gun on your left hip against a man?"

"I have."

Smith drank more whiskey and signaled the waiter for a refill. "Have you ever *killed* a man with that gun?"

"I'm afraid that I have."

"Many men?"

"More than I care to remember, Mr. Smith."

A young waiter in a dirty apron arrived with two glasses of whiskey. The waiter looked expectantly at Longarm, who thought, *Why not?*

"I'll have what Mr. Smith is ordering."

"That would be Old Barrister," the waiter told him. "Our best whiskey."

Old Barrister was a very good whiskey, one that Longarm always enjoyed but rarely felt he could afford. But this was on Smith's tab and it wasn't often that he had such an opportunity, so Longarm said, "Oh, why not? And young man, make mine a *double*."

"Very good," the waiter said with a happy smile, understanding full well what was taking place at his table. "And the lady and gentleman have ordered our finest steak, a filet mignon, for supper. It comes with . . ."

"I'll take it rare with whatever it comes with, and an excellent French wine would also be appropriate. Your very best cabernet, if you will, waiter."

"Of course!" The waiter looked very pleased, knowing his tip was going to be not large, but huge.

Mr. Smith tried to look delighted by this conversation, but Longarm could see beads of perspiration popping up all over his round, porcine face. No doubt that the man realized that he was getting shafted up the butt with a dry broomstick and there was little he could do about it but bear the pain and try to grin.

"To your business deal!" Lila said, taking her glass of whiskey and raising it high. "May you make a small fortune tomorrow, Mr. Smith!"

"Yes," Longarm said, wondering if the man was even from St. Louis, much less a feed dealer.

When the waiter brought Longarm a glass of whiskey, they all toasted again to good health and prosperity. Longarm was starting to enjoy himself immensely and looking forward to an outstanding supper on Mr. Smith's dime. If the man had been straight-up and honest with Lila, Longarm would not have taken advantage of his deceit. But since the man was using an alias and obviously trying to lure a far, far younger woman into his hotel bed, Longarm figured he was giving the salesman a very expensive but well deserved lesson in life.

Although slurring his words and getting rapidly drunk, Mr. Smith turned out to be a pretty good conversationalist and proved to be a real salesman in the cattle industry by giving Longarm his St. Louis business card. He also expounded on far too many cattle industry facts that neither Longarm nor Lila cared a fig about. By eleven o'clock that evening, the salesman was almost too drunk to talk, but Longarm made sure that Mr. Smith paid the supper bill and left a very generous tip on the linen dining room tablecloth.

"It has been a delight," Longarm said, meaning it because the beef steak had been far more tender and tasteful than expected and the whiskey had not been watered down to the slightest degree.

Smith heaved himself to his feet, belched, and then grabbed the back of his chair for support. With a loopy wave of his hand he then weaved his way out of the hotel's dining room without a single word of farewell or good night.

"I don't think he will be inviting either one of us to supper tomorrow night," Longarm told Lila after the man was gone.

She giggled. "I'm sure that he will not. Did you see the size of our dinner and drinks tab?"

"No."

"It was nearly *fifty* dollars." She shook her head. "I almost feel sorry for the poor man."

"He deserved it," Longarm said. "And besides, he did get the favor of our company tonight."

"Yes, he did get that," she agreed, emptying their third bottle of wine into their glasses.

"I have something from the office to give you," Longarm said, extracting the envelope from the inside of his coat pocket. "We took up a little collection after you left this morning."

She stared at the envelope. "I really can't accept charity. That's not what I came all the way to Denver expecting."

"Of course you didn't," Longarm assured her. "But everyone at the Marshal's office had heard of or even had met your famous father, and they all wanted to chip in a little to help. You'll find over fifty dollars in that envelope."

Lila took the envelope and appeared to be fighting off tears. "I can't tell you how much this means to us. And how very generous you are."

"It came from *everyone* at our office." Longarm patted her hand. "And tomorrow night, supper is on me, if you would like."

"That would be wonderful."

"May I escort you to your room, Miss Chandler?"

"Thank you."

Themselves a little bit tipsy, they left their table and then found Lila's hotel room. For a moment, Longarm thought he was going to be dismissed, but then the young woman smiled shyly and said, "Would you like to come inside, Marshal Long?"

"I would indeed!"

The moment they entered the room and closed the door, Lila was in his arms and they were kissing each other passionately. Longarm tore off her dress and then she tore off his shirt. They were removing each other's garments and laughing hysterically when they tripped and toppled to the rug. Longarm started to get up but Lila pulled him down to her and whispered, "Let's make love right here!"

"It's pretty hard."

"This rug can't be dirtier than my bedsheets," Lila whispered, kissing his bare chest and moving her hands down his hard body.

"You're probably right," he said, removing the last of her underclothes and staring at her lovely body.

"And besides," Lila panted, grabbing his manhood, "you'll go deeper inside of me on this hard floor."

That was all that Longarm needed to hear as he plunged into her warm honey pot. He sank his shaft to the hilt and she moaned with ecstasy and then wrapped her long legs around his back. For the next ten minutes they went at each other furiously until, finally, Longarm could stand the intensity of their lovemaking no longer and emptied his seed.

Lila shouted and bit him on the shoulder, then found her own soaring sweetness while dropping her long, shapely legs and pounding the floor with her bare heels.

Chapter 3

"Custis, you look like something my cat dragged through the door," Billy Vail said the next morning. "You're even limping. What happened to you last night?"

"Just scraped knees," Longarm said, not wanting to get into this discussion.

"Well, sit down and tell me about how you could have scraped your knees."

"Are you having a slow morning or something?" Longarm asked. "Why would you be interested in my damned knees?"

Billy grinned because it wasn't often that he was able to get under Longarm's skin. "Oh, I dunno. It's just that you're not only my best deputy marshal, you're also my most interesting."

"I'm glad that I amuse you most every morning," Longarm said, flopping down in a chair and rubbing his bloodshot eyes.

"Did you give that office donation to Miss Chandler after work?"

"I sure did."

Billy pursed his lips and studied Longarm intently. "What *else* did you give her last night?"

Longarm dropped his eyes to his lap and fidgeted for a moment before saying, "Never mind about that."

"You randy dog!"

"Dammit, Billy! How about telling that crabby secretary you hired to bring us in some hot, strong coffee?"

"Sure," Billy said. "I can see that you really need it this morning."

Longarm wasn't in any mood for small talk or for getting needled, so he sat slouched in the office chair and waited until the woman brought them coffee. She splashed a little on Longarm's lap, which didn't help his mood any, and he was sure that she did it on purpose. He decided right then and there that he and the new secretary were going to have to have a serious heart-to-heart talk.

"So," Billy continued when the woman was gone, "what's on your work schedule these days?"

"Nothing much." Longarm tasted his coffee and found it way too damned weak. "You gotta teach her to make a decent pot," he grouched.

"She's just trying to be thrifty and save the office a little money," Billy explained. "She heard about the tough spot the government is in financially, and I think she's afraid that being the last in the building hired, she might be the first fired."

"She ought to be the first fired, and I'll even do it for you."

"My, but you *are* in a foul mood today."

"Billy, I've been riding a desk for nearly two weeks and I'm about to go crazy looking at Wanted posters and trying to look busy pushing papers. I really need an assignment that will take me out of town next week."

"Why not this week?"

Longarm hedged his reply. He knew from long association with his boss that the man was smart and difficult to fool. "Well," he said, knowing it sounded suspicious, "I've got plans all the rest of this week."

"With Miss Lila Chandler, I'd bet."

Longarm said nothing.

"I've got some things that you could do in Denver the remainder of this week," Billy finally said. "You want to go over to the sheriff's office and see if he wants to send one of his deputies over here for training? You could teach him some of the new investigative stuff you learned at that meeting we had last month."

"Let someone else teach the locals."

Billy's smile slipped and he leaned forward on his desk. "What's *really* bothering you, Custis? Come on. We've been friends for too long to keep secrets."

Longarm sipped this weak coffee. "I have lots of secrets that I've never shared with you, Billy. Everyone has their private secrets. Even you."

"No!"

"Sure you do," Longarm said. "For example, you haven't told me how many times you and your wife make love each week, and if you do it anyplace besides your featherbed."

Billy's round face flushed with anger. "Dammit! What in the world has gotten into you? Did something go terribly wrong last night with you and Miss Chandler?"

"No," Longarm replied. "And you're right. Lovemaking with your wonderful wife is a secret that only the two of you need to share. But there is something really grinding at me, and it's my lousy government pay."

"Oh, that again," Billy said dismissively.

"Yeah, that again."

"Well, I really can't give you a raise for at least six months."

"And how much would it be?"

Billy thought for a moment. "Maybe ten dollars a month."

"That's about what I expected," Longarm said quietly. "And it doesn't cut it. The fact is that the Denver sheriff offered me a job at seventy-five bucks a month to start."

"You'd leave us for that small a raise?"

"I don't want to, but I might."

Billy steepled his fingers together and looked genuinely concerned. "I can't afford to lose someone with your talent and experience, Custis. I just can't."

"Then find the money to give me a decent pay raise!"

"I can't do that, either."

Longarm came to his feet and set his coffee cup down hard on Billy's desk. "Well, then I might just quit and go to work for the sheriff."

"Sheriff Art Beeson isn't the kind of man you would be happy working for. He's a tyrant and he's a politician. You and he would be butting heads inside of a week. And then he'd either fire you or you'd quit and want to come back here to work for me again. And then you know what?"

"What?" Longarm asked, suddenly curious.

"I would have a hell of a time re-hiring you because of the budget freeze we've got going with our department right now. And if I could hire you, it would be at even less pay than you're now earning. And wouldn't that be a fine kettle of stinking fish?"

"Yeah, it would," Longarm admitted. "But I do need more money."

"Why?" Billy demanded.

"I'd like to live a little better," Longarm told his boss. "Get a nicer set of rooms and maybe take a long-overdue vacation."

"And that 'overdue vacation' might be to Grants, New Mexico?"

"Yeah, it might," Longarm said, deciding just to come clean with his boss and friend. "I'd like to go there and see if maybe I can help out Lila and her family a mite. Kenyon Chandler is too good a man to have to struggle so hard for survival."

"Help them how?" Billy asked. "Miss Chandler and her family have a small cattle ranch. You're no cowboy and you'd make a lousy ranch hand. Can you throw a lariat?"

"You know I can't."

"Have you ever branded *anything*?"

"Nope."

"Then what are you thinking, Custis? You'd go crazy fixing fences, feeding and branding cows."

"Maybe I could do something more for the Chandler family."

Billy shook his head. "You're making no sense at all this morning. You know what I think?"

"No."

Billy pointed a finger at him. "I think you're smitten. Lovesick. I think you need to send Miss Chandler off on a train tomorrow afternoon and then take a couple of days off to sleep and rest those bruised knees."

Longarm had heard enough and he started for the door. "Billy," he said, "I never could hide much of anything real important from you and I've never really tried. But I'm tired of being poor and having to count pocket change. That Navajo boy needs a surgeon soon and that widow lady that we both send a little money to now and then in Wyoming is dying on the vine and her kids are probably underfed."

"You are not and never will be a saint, Custis. You're not the Pope sprinkling holy water and handing out wafers at Mass. You can't help everyone in financial straits."

"No, I can't," Longarm agreed. "But I want to do more than I'm doing, and I'm just frustrated as hell trying to figure out a way to do 'er."

"Getting a few more bucks working for Sheriff Art Beeson isn't going to make all that much of a difference."

"I know." Longarm was at Billy's door now. "I am thinking of doing something that will make some *real* money."

"Well, hellfire, Custis!" Billy exclaimed. "You've caught so many bank, train, and stagecoach robbers in this job that I'm sure you've figured out how to do better than them and get clean away with a lot of stolen money. If I were you, I'd pick a real busy bank and just . . ."

"Don't be a wiseass, Billy. Sarcasm has never been your winning style."

"And your style has never been to get rich."

"I would be a successful rich man, if it ever happened. I wouldn't go crazy or turn into a turdface like some of 'em do. I'd still treat people with respect . . . even you, Billy." Longarm was smiling now. "And I'd take you and your wonderful family out to dinner now and then and loan you money if you got into a tight fix. Yeah, I'd do that and help a lot of other people."

"Bullshit! More than likely you'd soon piss it all away on beautiful and cunning women," Billy said, also enjoying himself.

"Yeah, I might at that. But I sure would have a lot of fun first."

"You have a lot of fun *now*," Billy reminded him. "Was Lila as good as she looks?"

"Billy, a gentleman never tells."

"I suppose not, and I admire you for that," Billy said. "Besides, it's better for me to just use my rich imagination."

"You ought to daydream less and use your pecker more, Boss."

"Get out of here!"

"On my way," Longarm told him.

On Friday night Longarm took Miss Lila to the best restaurant in Denver and bought her the finest meal they had to offer. And wine, lots of good wine.

"I'll bet you wish that Mr. Smith was paying for this wonderful supper," Lila said as they were enjoying brandy and anticipating the lovemaking that would soon follow in this last night they shared.

"Naw," Longarm said. "Mr. Smith was pretty boring with all that cattle industry stuff he kept blabbing on about. And besides, we hit him up hard enough that first night at the Belleview Hotel."

"Yes," she agreed, "we did. And I'm concerned about all the money you've spent on me this week. Every night a different and expensive restaurant. Fine wines. The best whiskey in the house. Delicious desserts. Why, Custis, you could have hired the most expensive ladies of the night in Denver full time for what you've spent on this ranch girl from New Mexico."

"You're better than any lady of the night," he said. "And besides, I've never paid for one and never will."

"Really?"

"That's right."

She sipped her brandy. "I believe you. You're such a handsome man and a gentleman to boot. I'm sure that women just fall all over you at the office. When you walk down Colfax Avenue, I'll bet ladies run into street lamps, craning their necks around to watch your backside."

Longarm laughed and said, "Billy's new secretary and me sure don't admire each other much. She would very much like to club me in the backside, if she didn't know I would club her harder."

"I'll have to agree that the woman is very stern and proper looking. I'll bet she hasn't had a man between her legs in twenty years."

Longarm pretended to be mildly shocked. "Lila! How you talk sometimes."

"I'm a rancher and lawman's daughter," she said. "I've seen it all, and when I watch a bull mount a cow all I think about is that I hope the cow will have a nice calf in the spring that will get fat and make my family money."

"Have you ever been married?" he asked.

"Almost," she told him. "I fell in love twice. Both times ended badly. My first love was when I was sixteen. A cowboy, wild and free."

"So what happened to that one?"

She took a sip of her brandy and said, "My father shot him."

"Shot him?" Longarm asked with surprise.

"That's right. He caught us in the barn. Earnest Paine had my dress pushed up to my waist and his pants were down to his ankles. It would have been our first time, but because of my father catching us, it didn't happen."

"So your father actually *shot* the young cowboy?"

"Right though the buttocks. Sent him howling out the

door, tripping, screaming, and bleeding like a stuck pig. Poor Earnest managed to crawl onto his pony and race away. After that, nary a cowboy would even look at me again."

"I'm not a damn bit surprised!" Longarm shook his head. "And what happened to your second love? Did your father run him off, too?"

"No. My father liked Terrance Addington just fine. The trouble was that Terrance also liked all the young women around Grants just fine."

"Ahh, I understand."

"I was crazy in love with Terrance Addington. His family owned a big ranch not more than ten miles from our little one, and Terrance's people had money and respect. Terrance and I got engaged when I was twenty and we were set to be married in June when he suddenly died."

Longarm leaned forward, intent on the story. "Did your father kill him?"

"No, thank heavens. Terrance was caught in another man's bed with his pretty young wife. The husband busted in and shot both of them all to hell with a double-barreled shotgun."

"Holy cow," Longarm said. "That must have been a real mess."

"Oh, it was," Lila said, nodding. "It was the biggest event in Grants that year, and I alternated between feeling heartbroken and betrayed. They tried the husband in court, but the jury gave him a slap on the hand and a lot of people congratulated him because it turned out that

Terrance had been with plenty of other men's wives."

"I see."

"And so, Custis, I've been very unlucky at love. I haven't allowed myself to even think of getting serious about another man since Terrance betrayed me and died with his underpants on the floor."

"Not all men are that way."

"I know that." She reached out and touched his cheek. "But you're a bit like poor Terrance, aren't you, Custis? A real ladies' man."

"I stay away from the married ones," he said defensively. "No whores. No married women."

"You're honorable and adorable and I'll miss you terribly when I climb on that train tomorrow. I'll warn you right now that I'll probably cry."

"Maybe you won't need to cry."

"What's that mean?"

Longarm steepled his long fingers and looked her in the eye. "What would you say about me riding back to Grants with you?"

In reply, Lila Chandler let out a whoop of joy that filled the dining room. She lunged across the table, grabbed his face, and kissed him passionately.

"Does that mean you'd like me to go visit your family in Grants?" he asked, a bit embarrassed because everyone in the restaurant was staring.

"What do you think?"

"I think I'll buy a train ticket tomorrow." Then Longarm's face clouded. "But I'm a little short on cash."

"I've still got that money that your office donated."

"It was given to help your parents, not me."

"You'll be a big help to my parents, Custis. And to me. Please let me buy your ticket. We can make love in our sleeping compartment."

"I'd like that. But, Lila, it'll have to be a *round-trip* ticket."

"Of course. But you can always turn the ticket in for a refund, can't you?"

"Yeah," he confessed. "You can."

"Then it's settled!"

"Not quite," he said. "The southbound to Pueblo leaves at one o'clock in the afternoon, doesn't it?"

"Yes."

"That's perfect because it'll give me time to go into the office and tell my boss that I'm taking a short and sudden vacation to Grants, New Mexico."

"Will he be upset?"

"I'm sure that he will be, but he knows I need a change of pace and scenery. Besides, I'm too valuable to him for him to fire me."

"I like your boss," Lila said. "He's a very kind and generous man."

"I know. We've been friends for quite a while."

"Tomorrow, then!" Lila said, raising her glass in a salute.

"Tomorrow," Longarm repeated, raising his glass.

"And to many more tomorrows we can share."

Longarm smiled. He wondered if that would really be true.

Chapter 4

Billy Vail shook his head in resignation. "I guess I can't talk you out of this, huh?"

"Nope," Longarm said, "my mind is made up. I'm going to New Mexico with Lila and I'm gonna see what I can do to help her family."

"Are you thinking of . . . of marrying the young woman?"

"My thinking doesn't go that far or in that general direction," Longarm told his boss. "But I'm open to possibilities."

"I think you're making a huge mistake, Custis."

"I know you do, but my mind is set and I'll be boarding the train in a few hours."

"I could fire you," Billy said. "People can't just walk off their jobs and expect to be welcomed back if or whenever they please."

"Then fire me."

"No." Billy stood up from his desk and extended his

hand. "How many weeks' vacation time have you got saved up?"

Longarm thought for a moment. "A little more than three."

"Then take them on this trip. And if you stay longer than that, I'll finesse the paperwork so it looks like you're still a full-time marshal with pay."

"I thank you for that."

"You'll be back," Billy predicted. "I'm dead sure of it."

"I'm not."

"Then we'll just have to wait and see," Billy said. "At any rate, please give my regards to Marshal Chandler and his wife. I knew Kenyon when we were both actively working in the field, but I never had the pleasure of meeting his wife, Elsa. However, judging from her daughter, Elsa must be a lovely woman."

Longarm turned to go.

"Custis?"

"Yeah?" he asked, turning back to Billy.

"Tell my secretary to have a check cut for you. Three weeks' full salary. She'll come up with the right figure. Take the check and cash it before you leave Denver."

"That won't get you in trouble?"

"Not if no one knows about it."

"That secretary isn't to be trusted," Longarm told his boss.

"I trust her even if you don't. You'll need the money and I want you to have a good time. Don't give it all to the Chandlers, and make sure that you have a round-trip ticket in your hand before you leave this town."

Longarm didn't bother to tell the man that Lila was buying him that very ticket right now.

"So long, Billy."

"I'll see you in three weeks . . . four at the most."

Longarm nodded and headed out the door, wondering if he would ever see this office again.

Longarm had ridden the Denver and Rio Grande Railroad south many times. It was a fine little railroad and it hooked up down below Pueblo, Colorado, with the Santa Fe Railroad. He'd ridden both so many times over the years while tracking down killers and other criminals that he was quite a celebrity on both lines, and when they saw him boarding with Miss Lila Chandler, Longarm could see that their eyes were nearly popping with curiosity and envy.

"Got some lovely company this time, Marshal!"

"Yes, I do," Longarm said to the cheerful conductor, a short, middle-aged man whose name Longarm could not for the life of him ever remember.

"How far you going?"

"I'm going to visit with Miss Chandler's family near Grants."

"Ah, yes. We all remember her coming out last week. She's not only beautiful, she's a real sweetheart."

"I couldn't agree more," Longarm said.

"Separate sleeping compartments?"

Longarm nodded. As a gentleman, he would never compromise Lila's reputation. "Sure, but put them close together."

"Side by side," the conductor said with a wink.

"Perfect," Longarm said, slipping the man a generous tip.

The trip to New Mexico was a tonic for Longarm. He and Lila made love every night to the rocking of the rails. The weather stayed mild and the scenery, while not spectacular, was at least interesting.

"There are some fine cattle ranches between Albuquerque and Gallup," Lila was telling him. "It's a bit high for wintering livestock, but if you have a little summer range at the lower elevations, maybe down around Socorro or Las Cruces, it works out well."

"Does your family have any summer range in the lower country?"

"No," Lila said. "We rent some range and sell off the young steers before the winter comes. It's too expensive to feed them through a hard winter. But of course, now we only have a few cows and horses left."

"I'm sure that will change."

"I hope so. Our main goal is to save the ranch from being taken over by the bank."

"Are you far behind on your mortgage?"

"Several months. We have good water and grass, so the bank seems more than eager to step in and foreclose. If we lose the place, we'll never be able to buy another like it."

"Well," Longarm said, "then we just can't let that happen."

"No," she said quietly, "we just can't. I'm hoping for

a miracle, but I just don't know where it'll come from yet."

The next day, just outside of Albuquerque, they were sitting in the dining car, watching the mountains and valleys of northern New Mexico pass by, when a handsome young man in his late twenties came into the car and sat down at the next table.

"Good afternoon," he said in greeting.

"Good afternoon," Longarm said. "Traveling alone?"

"I am," the man said. "I'm going as far as Grants, New Mexico."

"So are we," Lila said. "My family has a small cattle ranch not far from that town. We've owned it for many years. My father was a United States Marshal but we always had the ranch as our main source of family income. Now, Father is retired and we're ranching full-time."

The young man looked at Longarm. "So you're both going home from someplace?"

"Denver," Longarm said. "I'm just visiting."

"He might be staying longer than he thinks," Lila said, squeezing Longarm's hand.

The young man nodded. "Never been to Denver, but I hear it's a great town to visit and it's getting to be quite a big city."

"That's true," Longarm said. "It's growing fast."

"Are you also a cattleman?"

"No," Longarm said. "I'm a United States Deputy Marshal. Name is Custis Long and this is Miss Lila Chandler."

"Are you out here on lawman's business?" the man asked.

"I'm on vacation," Longarm told him.

"Well, Custis, my name is Ned Corey, and I'm sure you'll enjoy New Mexico. I'm from up in Raton. My father owns a saloon there and I'm a small-town newspaper editor. I print a weekly called the *Raton Reader*. I've built the circulation up to over a hundred sales in regular copies, but even so I'm barely covering my expenses. To pay my bills, in my spare time I work for my father at his saloon doing pretty much whatever needs doing. That's also where I pick up a lot of my newspaper stories. You know how people talk after a few glasses of beer or whiskey."

"That sounds like a good arrangement for you, Ned," Lila told him.

"It's all right. Like most fellas, I have a difficult time working for my father. He's harder on me than anyone else that works for him at the saloon. But I draw the line when it comes to cleaning those brass spittoons."

It was meant to be a joke and they all laughed.

"Fathers can be like that," Lila said. "I work with my folks on our cattle ranch from early spring until after the fall roundup. In the winter, I try to get a paying job in Grants to pick up some extra money, but things are slow these days and cash money is always in short supply."

"I know," Ned agreed. "My weekly newspaper is hardly breaking even and, if it weren't for the family saloon, well, I don't know what I'd do. But all that may be changing soon."

"Oh?" Longarm asked, raising his eyebrows in question.

"I'm afraid that I can't talk about it."

"That's perfectly fine," Lila said. "We all have our secrets."

"Let's have some whiskey," Longarm said. "It's on me."

"In that case, I'll accept," Ned said with a laugh.

After that, the afternoon passed quickly as they shared stories and got acquainted. By evening, as it neared suppertime, Ned was a little tipsy, which surprised Longarm, considering the man had grown up working in his father's saloon. Longarm and Lila ordered a chicken dinner and Ned told the waiter he'd like the same. They had a bottle of white wine and then a brandy as it grew later and the other diners left for their sleeping compartments.

"We'll be in Grants around midnight," Longarm told the newspaperman after he paid for all three meals and their drinks. "Ned, do you have you a place in mind to stay?"

"Not really," Ned confessed. "I'm hoping there's a cheap and decent hotel near the train station with a vacant room I can rent for a few days while I see to my business."

"There will be," Lila promised him. "We'll be staying there for the rest of the night, too. Tomorrow I'll find someone to take us out to our ranch."

"This is pretty rugged country," Ned mused. "Miss Chandler, have you ever heard of gold being found in these parts?"

She shrugged. "Now and then there's a find. No huge strikes, but there is gold in this country. Silver, too."

"Any strikes lately?" Ned asked.

"Not that I know of," she said. "Why do you ask?"

Ned Corey drained his glass of whiskey and studied both Longarm and Lila closely for a moment. "You have both been very hospitable and generous to me," Ned told them just before it was time to retire. "And I'm going to share a secret I will ask you to keep."

"We'll keep your secret," Longarm promised, stifling a yawn.

Ned Corey leaned over the table and whispered, "I'm here to strike it rich at a place called Skull Mountain."

"Skull Mountain?"

"Shhhh!" Corey hissed, looking around the dining car, which by now was empty except for an impatient waiter. "Don't tell anybody, but I have a prospector's map showing me where there's a rich gold mine."

Longarm and Lila exchanged amused glances, then Longarm turned back to the obviously inebriated young newspaperman and said, "Ned, if I were you, I'd keep quiet about the map. Could be dangerous if the wrong kind of people heard about it and thought it might be the real thing."

"It is the real thing!" Ned hiccupped, excused himself, and said, "But the trouble is that I don't even know where Skull Mountain is located! And I don't know a thing about mining or prospecting. Worse yet, I don't have the money to go out there and find and then dig up any gold."

"I'm sure that you'll figure out something," Longarm said, humoring the young man. "But keep it under your hat."

"Oh, I sure will." Ned shook his head as if to clear it of cobwebs and said, "Lila, have you ever been on Skull Mountain?"

"No, because it's about ten miles north of our family ranch. I've ridden up that way and have seen it in the distance. But I've never actually gone there. I can tell you that it's really big and tall."

"Aw, shoot," Ned said. "I was hoping it was a *little* mountain."

"Well," Lila said, "it's not. You would have to ride at least a full day to circle Skull Mountain. There's probably snow still on its peak."

"Where do you think it got its name?" Ned asked. "I mean, Skull Mountain sounds pretty dark and deadly, doesn't it?"

"They call it Skull Mountain because an early fur trapper found three skulls on the mountain and they were encased in the rusted helmets of Spanish conquistadores. As the story goes, there were also swords, metal breastplates, and two rotted leather pouches filled with several pure gold nuggets. At least, that's the legend that I was told."

"Then you see!" Ned crowed. "There *is* gold on Skull Mountain!"

But Lila shook her head. "I think that the story has been proven false because over the years prospectors have come to Skull Mountain hunting for the source of those supposed gold nuggets and all of them have gone away empty-handed."

Ned leaned forward and whispered, "That's not quite true, Lila."

"Oh?"

Ned's eyes narrowed and his voice dropped so low that it was difficult to hear the man over the hammering of the train. "Do you both swear to keep this a secret?"

Lila and Longarm both nodded.

"All right, then, I'm going to trust you with the secret that brings me here."

Ned signaled the bored waiter to bring them all another round of brandies. "I'm paying for this round," he said.

When the drinks arrived, Ned waited until the waiter was gone and then he said, "Last winter during a blizzard, a dying and half-frozen prospector staggered into my newspaper office. He wanted to know if I would pay him for what he called 'the biggest story of your lifetime.' Of course, I thought he was a little crazy and told him that I didn't have any money to spare on wild tales."

"How much money did he want for his story?" Lila asked.

"Enough money to stay drunk and warm until he passed away. He had the consumption and his lungs were shot. I could tell that he wouldn't last more than a few days."

Ned sighed and then continued. "Besides his dire circumstances, there was something about the prospector that moved me deeply. He was old and ugly, but I sensed that he was basically a good and honest man. He told me that he had children back East and asked me if I might write to them of his passing, and I promised him that I would do my best in that regard. This seemed to mean a lot to him, and when I brought a bottle of whiskey over from my father's saloon, he was most grateful."

"Every prospector has a story about a secret gold strike or mine," Longarm said. "I'm glad you gave the old man comfort, but I think you were probably lied to."

"That's what I would have thought," Ned told them, "but how can you turn a dying and lonely old man away? And besides, I thought he might have a fine tale for me to write about in my paper. And so I promised the old man that if his story proved to be true, then his name would forever be written in the history of the New Mexico Territory."

"And he was willing to settle for that?" Lila asked.

"Not entirely," Ned told them. "The dying prospector's name was Joshua Bixby, and I know that because he gave me the names and addresses of his two sons living back East. Joshua said that he wanted to spend his last hours drinking and remembering happier times."

"I wonder why he came to your newspaper office?" Longarm mused.

"I'm sure that someone had told him that my father owned the biggest saloon in Raton and Joshua had gotten it into his old head that I could probably talk my father into giving him a steady supply of whiskey. And when the old man showed me a gold nugget the size of a robin's egg, I suddenly became a believer."

"Wait," Lila said. "If Joshua Bixby had a gold nugget that size, why did he need any help from you? He could have sold the nugget and bought all the whiskey he could drink until he died."

"You're right, but Joshua knew that if he showed anyone the nugget, they would waylay him when he was drunk and beat him almost to death to find out exactly where he prospected that big gold nugget."

Longarm saw the way of it now. "And so, Ned, you saw his gold nugget and had a heart-to-heart talk with your father."

"That's right." Ned smiled sadly. "My father has heard so many gold strike stories that I knew he'd never believe a word of what Bixby had to say unless the old prospector showed him the nugget."

"Which he did?"

"Joshua gave me the nugget to show to my father. At the same time he drew me a map of the strike he'd made on Skull Mountain. Only I knew my father would just say the whole story was a lie and then he'd want to keep the nugget for himself."

"So you said nothing to your father?" Lila asked.

"That's right," Ned told them. "My father isn't what you would call an honest man. I've learned that through some hard and painful lessons."

"Then," Longarm suggested, "you must still have the

nugget and the map that Joshua Bixby drew up before he died."

"I do," Ned said. "I stayed with Joshua until the end, and I have to tell you, I heard some wild stories. The old man died drunk and in his sleep, just like he wanted. He was warm and dry and I cared for him to the end and then made sure that he'll have a decent burial when the ground thaws next spring."

"And was the nugget pure gold?" Lila asked.

"I think so. Want to see it?"

"Sure!" Lila told him.

Ned looked around secretively, then reached into his pocket and drew out a clean white handkerchief. He placed it on the table between them and slowly unfolded it to reveal the gold nugget. "See," he whispered, "big as a robin's egg."

Longarm reached out and hefted the nugget. Without a doubt it was heavy and solid gold.

"What do you think it's worth?" Ned blurted.

Longarm shrugged his broad shoulders and looked to Lila, who also shrugged.

Ned looked disappointed. "No idea?"

"If I had to guess," Longarm said, choosing his words carefully, "I'd say it's worth about five or six hundred dollars."

"That's what poor Joshua told me the day before he died."

Longarm was impressed. "Well," he said, "it appears that you might be on to something more than just another hoax."

"Sure I am!" Ned exclaimed. "And I've got Mr. Bixby's map, but it isn't a good one. Not good at all. The old man was dead drunk and dying when he drew it for me, and even though I pleaded for him to be accurate, I doubt that he was. Joshua's hand shook, and he was forgetting at the time."

"So what are you going to do?" Lila asked.

Ned threw up his hands and said, "I'm going to go to Skull Mountain and spend however much time I need to find Mr. Bixby's gold strike. Then I'm going to file a claim and become a very rich man."

"Well," Longarm said, giving the nugget back to the newspaperman, "I hope you pull it off."

"Me, too," Lila said.

"Thank you." Ned cleared his throat. "But I can't do it alone, and that's where you both come into it."

"Us?"

"Why not?" Ned Corey asked. "Custis, you're a lawman, and I'll need protection both for my person and for the rich mining claim I intend to file somewhere on Skull Mountain. And you, Lila, know the lay of the land and can provide the horses and things we'll need to hunt for and locate Joshua Bixby's gold mine."

"Now, wait a minute," Longarm said. "I'm on vacation, and Lila is . . ."

"Is *interested*," she said, giving Longarm a determined look. "Ned, I'll be very honest with you, since you've been the same with us. The sad truth is that my family is about to lose our ranch and maybe this . . . this gold find is exactly the miracle we need to get through these tough times. But there's something that you won't like hearing."

"And that would be?"

"Custis and I would expect to be *equal* partners with you."

"*Equal* partners?"

"That's right," Lila told him. "Without us, you don't have a prayer of finding the gold, and even if you did you'd never live to spend your mining fortune."

"You sure are asking me to make a hard bargain," Ned complained.

"It's a hard world," Lila said. "And I'm trying to save my dear father and mother from being evicted from a ranch they worked for most of their lives. And Custis is due to find a new profession."

Longarm said nothing. He didn't believe in forcing a man into a hard decision such as Ned was now facing.

"Waiter!" Ned called out. "Bring us another round of brandies!"

Ned wrung his soft hands that were stained by printer's ink. He stared out the window until the drinks arrived and then he sighed heavily.

"Ned," Longarm told him, "you can't do this without help, and I'm sure that there are plenty of people in Grants who will tell you that they'll take far less than an equal share."

"There probably are," Ned agreed. "But could I trust them?"

"That's the risk you'd have to take," Lila told the man.

"Well," Ned decided, "it's a risk I'd rather not take. Custis, you're a good man with a gun, I take it?"

"I can handle any trouble that would come our way."

"And you, Lila. Your family is in bad financial straits and you were looking for a miracle in order to save your ranch?"

"That's the long and short of it," Lila said.

"All right then," Ned told them, coming to a sudden decision. "If you will join me in this venture, we'll see if we can find Joshua Bixby's gold mine and all become wealthy."

"Let's drink to that," Longarm said.

And so they did, and the deal was done with a toast and handshakes all around the table.

Chapter 5

It was well past midnight when Longarm, Lila, and their new partner, Ned Corey, climbed down from the train in Grants, New Mexico. The night was filled with stars and a big, golden crescent moon.

"We can stay the rest of this night at the Pinto Pony Hotel," Lila said as Longarm and Ned gathered their traveling suitcases and bags. "I know the owner and he won't mind if we just pick a key off the board and leave him a note. We can settle the bill tomorrow morning."

"How much will it cost?" Ned asked. "I mean, I could just sleep in the lobby for the rest of the night. I'm an early bird and I really need to save every penny I can."

"I'm sure that will be fine," Lila told the young newspaperman. "The hotel owner's name is Homer Monroe and he's a good friend of my family. When my father was a United States Marshal, he did a few favors for Homer and the man has always been good to us and

our friends. He'll give you a very reasonable room rate
tomorrow night, Ned."

"I'm glad to hear that. How soon can we get started
for Skull Mountain?"

"How about the day after tomorrow?" Lila suggested.
"That will give Custis and me time to get to the ranch
and get things put together for the journey."

"How much in the way of provisions will we be need-
ing?" Ned asked. "I was hoping it won't cost too much."

"Let's pack for a week on Skull Mountain," Lila said.
"We'll bring you a saddle horse and I'll also bring a
couple of pack animals with food, blankets, and grain
for the animals. If we don't find anything after a week,
we can decide then if we want to come back here, re-
provision, and then go back out."

"I'll want to," Ned told them. "There's a fortune to be
found on Skull Mountain and we shouldn't give up, even
if it takes all summer."

"We'll see," Longarm told the earnest young newspaperman.

"We'll need some prospecting tools," Ned told them.
"You know, picks and shovels and whatever else prospectors use to poke around for gold."

"We've already got those at our ranch," Lila told him.
"Don't buy anything like that or you'll just raise suspicion. If anyone asks . . . and they will . . . tell them that
you're a reporter who is on vacation and wants to take a
little packing trip up to Chaco Canyon to see the ancient
Indian ruins."

"There are Indian ruins up toward Skull Mountain?"

Lila nodded. "Some of the most extensive and interesting in the entire Southwest. Lots of people go up there to look at them and see the ancient writings on the stone walls. No one knows what they mean or even how long they've existed, but it's fun to imagine the ancient Indian culture and the people who left so many ruins and stone writings, which the archaeologists call pictographs and petroglyphs."

"If Skull Mountain isn't too far away from Chaco Canyon, I'd kind of like to visit that place."

But Longarm shook his head. "If we're going to hunt for a fortune in gold, let's stick to the business at hand. Ned, after we're all rich, you can come back and see Chaco Canyon any time you want and do it in style."

"He's right," Lila said. "There are even outfitters starting to take tourists up to the ruins at Chaco Canyon. What we want to do is to go up to Skull Mountain without raising any interest or suspicion. So whatever you do, don't get drunk in a saloon and confide about old Joshua Bixby's gold nugget and treasure map."

Ned looked a bit hurt and offended. "I'm not a complete fool, Lila. Of course I'll keep everything to myself."

"That's good to hear," Longarm told the man as they walked up Grants's dark and empty main street, which was mostly lined with cottonwood trees and businesses built of stone and adobe. Longarm had never before left the Santa Fe train to actually walk around this old railroad town, but now in the moonlight he had the impression that Grants, New Mexico, was neither thriving nor prosperous. To Longarm it appeared to be like dozens of other railroad towns that he'd seen, and had it not been on the busy Santa Fe Railroad line, it would probably have wilted and eventually faded away.

"I have to tell you that I'm too excited to sleep," Ned said as they neared the Pinto Pony Hotel. "The idea of becoming rich . . . or even a little affluent . . . is something that I've always dreamed about but never really thought would happen."

"Don't spend that gold money in your mind," Longarm advised. "You admitted that Joshua Bixby's map was written as he was dying and is hardly accurate."

"I know. I know," the newspaperman said. "But I did question him very carefully and I took notes."

"And you brought the notes with you?" Lila asked.

"Yes. But a lot of the main facts about what the old prospector said can only be found in my head. I thought that was the safest place for the most important details. I knew coming here that I was going to be taking a big risk, and I figured that someone might be able to steal the map and even the nugget, but they'd never be able to steal the critical details that I carry around in my mind."

"That's good thinking," Longarm said. "My advice would be to stay as much to yourself as possible until we come for you ready to ride off. If anyone gets the slightest inclination that there's gold on Skull Mountain, it'll cause a gold rush, and that's the very last thing the three of us need.

"This town is bigger than I thought," Longarm said as they trudged up the darkened main street.

"It's had quite a history," Lila said. In the next few moments she told Longarm and Ned that the handsome two-story hotel where they were staying had originally been called the Santa Fe Hotel, but then it had burned to the ground twice. Not being an entirely stupid man, Homer Monroe had bought the fire-gutted hotel when it was just a heap of smoldering ashes. Because of its good location and proximity to the railroad, he'd rebuilt the hotel using fireproof sandstone and adobe mortar for its external walls. The sandstone and mortar had blended over the years, and because of hard snow and rains, the hotel now had a unique spotty appearance composed mostly of reds, yellows, and whites; so the building was renamed the Pinto Pony Hotel.

Now it was very well maintained and boasted an excellent restaurant, bar, and sixteen rooms catering to a much higher-class clientele than most of its newer competitors. The hotel's lobby was decorated in keeping with its unusual name. The floor tiles were red, yellow, and white to match the outside walls. The hanging crystal chandeliers were impressive, and the big easy chairs and sofas that circled a massive rock fireplace were upholstered with the colorful hides of spotted Texas longhorn cattle. The fireplace was still glowing warm with smoldering logs and was inviting to late-night arrivals coming in off the railroad.

"Nice," Ned said, looking around at the tasteful decor and handsome appointments. "Looks kinda expensive, though."

"It won't be for you," Lila assured him. "If you want

to stay tonight for free, I'd suggest you put your bags behind the registration desk and simply remove your shoes and stretch out on that big cowhide-covered couch nearest the fireplace."

Just when she finished saying that, the grandfather clock in the lobby chimed one, causing Longarm to yawn. "Let's get a room," he said, tired of travel and conversation.

"All right," Lila said, going around the registration desk and selecting a key. "Room 102 is empty and just down the hall."

"I'll take my own room," Longarm told her in a voice plenty loud enough to be overheard by Ned Corey.

Lila gave him a questioning glance, but Longarm ignored it. This was Lila's hometown, and she was well known and respected in Grants. If he and Lila shared the same room in this hotel tonight or any other night, Longarm was willing to bet that all of Grants would be buzzing with gossipers. And Longarm, always the gentleman, would not allow that to happen.

"You can have Room 201," Lila said, selecting a key to a room obviously on the second floor. "That way no one can possibly gossip about us."

"Sounds good."

Ned was already removing his shoes. "I wonder what time Mr. Monroe or someone he employs will arrive this morning to open this place up for business."

"I don't know," Lila told him. "I've never been down here in the lobby at that early of an hour."

"Well," the newspaperman said, also yawning, "I hope it isn't too early."

Longarm took his key and kissed Lila on the lips, saying, "Good night. See you in the morning for breakfast."

"Aren't you even going to be the gentleman and carry my suitcase to my hotel room door?" she said.

"Of course I will," Longarm told her.

When they reached the door, Lila put her arms around his neck and gave him a much more passionate kiss. "Are you sure you can't come in for just a few minutes?"

"I'd better not," he decided. "You know that our young friend will still be awake and listening for my footsteps to climb those stairs."

"Yes, I suppose that's true. What do you think about all this gold business on Skull Mountain?"

"I honestly don't know what to think," Longarm told her. "We saw the nugget, but I'm sure you're as aware as I am that he was not about to show us the prospector's map."

"No, he wasn't. Can we trust him?"

"I think so." Longarm leaned up against the wall, keeping his voice low so that Ned Corey couldn't overhear this conversation. "The fact of the matter is that he really needs us, Lila. If we're to believe him, the young man is almost broke. I don't know how he thought he was going to go off to Skull Mountain without buying a horse and provisions."

"Me neither," she said. "And the other thing is that we hold most of the hole cards in this game."

"Those being?"

"I have the horses and equipment and you have the

savvy to keep someone from coming up and killing us for the gold . . . if we find it."

"I'm going to need a Winchester repeating rifle," Longarm said. "I was hoping that your father would have one I could borrow."

"He has several and all the ammunition you'll need. If it weren't for my mother's poor health, I'm sure he'd insist on coming along with us."

"Might be better if he didn't," Longarm said. "This could be a tough hunt."

"My father is still tough as an old leather boot."

"I'm sure that he is," Longarm said quickly, "but all the same, I think that the three of us are less likely to attract attention. Also, it will be good to have your father at the ranch as support . . . if things go sour."

"How would they do that?"

Longarm shrugged. "Lila, if there's one thing I've learned, it's that out in wild country you had better expect the worst and hope for the best. If something can go wrong, it will go wrong."

"My," she said, "that's a very pessimistic outlook, Marshal Custis Long. I'm surprised to hear such talk from a seasoned lawman like you."

"I've survived on hunts because I've always expected the worst and been prepared for it. And to tell you the truth, I don't trust young Ned to keep his mouth shut. He opened up to us after a few drinks and I think there's every chance that he will do the same in some saloon tomorrow."

"He's smarter than that."

"Oh," Longarm said, "he's smart enough. But the fact is that sometimes fellas who think they're smarter than the next guy get outsmarted themselves. And I wouldn't be surprised if that happens."

"I hope it doesn't. There are some real tough men in this town. Men who would do most anything for a few dollars, let alone a fortune in gold."

"That's why I need a rifle."

"I'll bring one, too," she told him. "I'm actually a very good shot."

"I can believe that."

"Good night," she said, kissing him once more and then opening her door and disappearing.

Longarm headed up the stairs to his own room, calling out as the passed through the hotel lobby, "Good night, Ned."

"Good night, Custis."

"Hope you sleep well on that cowhide couch."

"Me, too. But with this gold nugget in my pocket, I'm not likely to sleep much at all."

"If you want, I'll keep it safe for you tonight."

"No, thanks!"

"I kinda thought you'd say that."

"It's not that I don't trust you."

"Of course you don't," Longarm told the man. "We only met a short while ago, so you hardly know me."

"You're really a federal officer of the law, aren't you?"

"Yep."

"Then that's good enough for me!"

Longarm smiled in the semi-darkness as he climbed the stairs and found his room. Tomorrow he would meet Lila's famous father and her ailing mother, as well as have a look at the modest cattle ranch that they had put together and were in danger of losing to a local bank. And after that, well, Longarm would, for the first time in his life, go searching for gold.

All in all, he thought, the next couple of weeks were going to be very interesting.

Chapter 6

Longarm slept a little late the next morning and by the time that he got up, shaved, dressed, and went downstairs to the hotel's little dining room, Lila and Ned were already finishing their breakfast.

"Well, well," Lila chided him, "look who finally got out of bed."

"I was tired," Longarm said, taking a seat at the table. "I hope you both slept as soundly as I did."

"Not me," Ned replied. "I didn't sleep a wink. And not long before daybreak the cook came stomping in through the front door, whistling as if he were a fool in love. I was dozing on that couch, trying to save my back from getting knotted up, when the man began to feed the fireplace with logs. Of course, he saw me and wanted to talk."

"Of course." Lila laughed. "That would have been Otis. He's worked for Homer Monroe for the past five years and he's one of the best cooks you'll ever find."

Ned nodded. "That was a fine breakfast we just enjoyed. Thank you, Lila."

"My pleasure," she replied, sounding as if she really meant it. She turned to Longarm. "I'm going to show Ned around Grants and then I'll hire us a man to deliver you and me to our family's KC Ranch. I expect that you'll be finished with your breakfast by the time I get that done."

"I'll do my best," Longarm replied.

"I'm eager to see my parents," Lila confided to them both. "They weren't a bit in favor of me going to Denver all by myself to visit Marshal Billy Vail. But now I can tell them that everything turned out even better than expected."

"Are you going to tell them about Joshua Bixby's gold strike up on Skull Mountain?" Ned asked.

"Of course! After all, we'll be riding my father's horses and using a lot of his camping gear during our hunt."

"Yeah," Ned said. "I'm sure he'd never believe the Chaco Canyon story."

Lila's smile faded. "That's not the *point*, Ned. The real point is that I would never lie to my father."

"I meant no offense."

"Then none taken," she said, getting up from the table and leaving some money for their meals. "Custis, I'll see you in about an hour or perhaps a little bit longer."

"I'll get your suitcase and my bags and be waiting in the lobby," he promised.

When they had left, Longarm ordered a large breakfast of ham, potatoes, and pancakes. He was hungry and thought it likely that he would not eat before suppertime. His breakfast soon arrived, and by then he was already working on his second cup of black coffee.

"Good morning," a heavyset man with muttonchop whiskers said in greeting. "I'm Homer Monroe and I understand that you, Lila, and some other fella that slept in the lobby came in late last night."

"More like early this morning," Longarm said, rising from his chair and introducing himself.

"Mind if I join you and have a cup of coffee?"

"Hell no. You own the place, don't you?"

"I do indeed." Homer Monroe took a seat across the table from Longarm, and when his coffee was poured, he sipped it, smacked his porcine lips with satisfaction, and pronounced, "That's a fine cup of coffee! I insist on making sure that my guests have an excellent cup or two of morning coffee. My way of thinking is that if you start your day off right, then it'll stay right. Yes sir. And I hear that the Santa Fe serves lousy coffee in the train's dining car."

"Your coffee is much better than the Santa Fe pours," Longarm assured the man.

"Glad to hear that!" Homer Monroe leaned back in his seat. "I spoke to Miss Chandler this morning and that nice newspaperman she was having breakfast with. He seems like a fine young fellow. Said his father owns a saloon in Raton and he's got a weekly newspaper."

"That's right."

"Is Lila sweet on the young fella?"

Longarm chuckled. "I think and hope that I'm the one that she's sweet on, Mr. Monroe."

"Homer. That's all I go by. So it's you, a Denver marshal, that Lila has taken a fancy too, eh?"

"I suppose so."

"Well, Marshal, I just hope and I'll assume that you're a decent and honorable man when it comes to that lady. She's already been hurt and disappointed too often."

"So she told me," Longarm said. "And don't worry, I'm honorable."

"Glad to hear that! Are you going out to the KC Ranch this morning to meet her parents?"

"I am." Longarm was beginning to wonder why this man was asking him so many personal questions.

"Good. I wanted to have a little chat with you about Kenyon Chandler. He and I are longtime friends. We've drank a lot of liquor together, shared our joys and sorrows. In short, we're the best of friends."

"All right," Longarm said. "That's good."

"Yes, but Kenyon is a troubled man these days. Deeply troubled. And I'm worried half sick about his health."

"Lila told me that he was in poor health and her mother's health was even worse."

"That's true. Mrs. Kenyon is very near death and when she goes . . . and that could be any day . . . I think that Kenyon will snap and do something awful."

"Like what?" Longarm asked.

"I don't know. But I'm sure that if Lila told you about

her parents' failing health, she's also told you that they are staring foreclosure right in the face."

"Yes, she told me that."

"You know, Marshal, when a man like Kenyon Chandler is pushed too hard up against a wall, he is likely to do something pretty drastic . . . even violent."

"Why don't you get to the point, Homer?"

"All right, I will," the hotel owner said. "I think that when Mrs. Chandler passes, Kenyon is going to go completely off the deep end. You see, he blames Grants Savings and Loan, and more specifically its owner, John Jacob, for all the financial troubles that he is now facing."

"And do you think that blame is justified?"

"Yes, I do," Homer said without hesitation. "John Jacob started his bank only six years ago and he came to Grants with a lot of money. Over the past six years, he's loaned money to nearly all of us, and at a damn steep rate of interest."

"If the interest was too high," Longarm responded, "neither you, Kenyon, nor anyone else should have taken a loan out at the man's bank."

"There's something that I haven't told you yet, and that is that the bank's loan papers contained some very fine print and fancy words that meant that the loans rates were adjustable, always upward. When most of us found out about that, we were furious with Jacob and paid off our loans no matter how difficult it was. But some people just couldn't do that because of circumstances totally beyond their control."

"People like former Marshal Kenyon Chandler."

"That's right," Homer said. "And so one by one, the Grants Savings and Loan began to swallow up businesses, homes, ranches, and other real estate. It was like an octopus reaching out with its tentacles to all parts of this town and its people. And today, Jacob and his bank are strangling the town and calling all the shots. The banker is also a lawyer, and he's plenty shrewd and totally heartless. He decides who gets elected on the city council and to the marshal's office, and even the mayor is in his hip pocket."

"Sounds pretty unhealthy to me," Longarm said.

"It is damned unhealthy! Why, this hotel is one of the few prospering establishments neither owned or mortgaged to the local bank. I've even thought about selling out and moving on, but no one in their right mind would buy me out, given the circumstances."

"So back to the original point of discussion," Longarm said. "You are worried about Kenyon Chandler doing violence, but not against himself . . . against John Jacob, banker and swindling lawyer."

"That's exactly right," Homer said. "Many are the nights when Kenyon has had a bit too much of my best whiskey and threatened to kill the man. And since he doesn't think he is long for this world, Kenyon has very little to lose."

Longarm threw up his hands. "I appreciate you forewarning me about all this, but I really don't see how it concerns me, Homer."

"If you care for Kenyon's daughter and her future, then it *directly* concerns you."

"What would you have me do?" Longarm asked bluntly.

"I'd like you to get to know Kenyon and, if he intends to kill John Jacob, talk him out of it."

"I don't even know Mr. Chandler," Longarm said. "Why would he listen to me, a stranger?"

"If Kenyon believes that his daughter is serious about you, then he might listen. Also, you're a federal marshal, and that will carry a hell of a lot of weight in his mind."

"I'm a deputy marshal and I really doubt that my opinion or advice will carry any weight with the man."

"Just listen, and if he's talking about shooting John Jacob, then try to talk him out of it. I sure would hate to see my old friend and such a great lawman hung by the neck from a tree."

"Me, too," Longarm said, thinking of how hard his boss, Billy Vail, would feel about such a horrible fate for his old friend, Kenyon Chandler, not to mention what it would do to poor Lila.

"Then you'll at least try to reason with Kenyon?"

"I will," Longarm promised. "Even though I doubt it will make a bit of difference."

"You know, you remind me of Kenyon when he was quite a bit younger," Homer said. "He was tall once, like you. Strong as an ox and as fearless as a catamount. He was the best man I ever knew."

"That's high praise for your friend."

"He deserves that and more. Kenyon saved my bacon a time or two, and I've always tried to pay him with my loyal friendship and free drinks when he comes into my saloon." Homer stood up to leave. "Find out what Kenyon is intending to do and try to help him, please."

"I will."

"Thank you, and I hope that you and Lila find some happiness out on the KC Ranch. There isn't any of it out there right now."

"I understand," Longarm said, afraid that he really did.

Chapter 7

"The man who owns the local livery let me use this buckboard and old horse to get us to the ranch," Lila announced as she drove up to the Pinto Pony Hotel, where Longarm was waiting with their bags. "I told him we'd be coming back to town tomorrow or the next day and would return the horse and wagon."

Longarm tossed the bags into the buckboard. He looked closely at the thin swaybacked horse and said, "Do you really think that old boy will make it to your ranch and back pulling this wagon? He looks like he's about ready to ship out any minute now."

"He'll make it," Lila assured him.

Ned Corey was sitting up on the wagon's seat beside Lila and said, "Lila suggested I come out with you both to the ranch and stay. Might as well visit her folks as wait here at the hotel."

Longarm raised his eyebrows in question, but Lila said, "My parents will enjoy Ned's visit. And that way, he won't be at such loose ends until we come back to buy provisions."

"Sounds fine to me," Longarm said, although for some reason he was a little disappointed. He'd wanted to spend time with Lila and her parents alone, but maybe Lila was thinking that this way a bored and lonesome Ned wouldn't drink too much and let his tongue wag.

Ned jumped down from the wagon. "I'll get my bag out of the hotel and be right back."

"So why did you change your mind about him?" Longarm asked when they were alone.

"I didn't want Ned sitting around here cooling his heels and maybe drinking and talking too much."

Longarm nodded. "Makes sense, I suppose."

She looked down at him. "You sound a little annoyed. You're not jealous of Ned, are you?"

"Me?"

"Yeah," she said, grinning, "you."

"I'm not the jealous kind."

She winked at him. "Not until now, maybe."

Longarm shook his head and climbed up into the wagon. "Ned can sit in the back and let his heels hang."

"Of course he can," she said.

A few minutes later, Lila snapped the lines and the old bay horse stumbled off down Grants's main street. As they passed the bank, a nattily dressed man in his late thirties stepped out on the boardwalk and waved. He was a dandy, with a derby hat cocked jauntily on his head and a long black cigar sticking out of the corner of his mouth. Of average height, his jowls almost had a shine from a fresh barbershop shave, and the tips of his long black mustache were waxed and curved upward like the horns of a bull.

"That's John Jacob, the wealthiest man in town," Lila said, not even bothering to wave back at the handsome banker. "He's the one that intends to foreclose on our KC Ranch just as soon as possible."

"He looks like a shark," Longarm said, although he'd actually never seen a shark. "And Homer Monroe said he's ruthless."

"He is. And just for your information, he wants me to marry him."

"What?" Longarm craned his head around and looked back at the banker, who wore an almost mocking grin. "He is foreclosing on your ranch and at the same time he's trying to get you to marry him?"

"That's right. And he's persistent, too. He told me that if I married him, he'd make me a rich man's wife, take me to faraway places, and allow my parents to stay on the KC Ranch until they died. But of course I told him to go bugger himself."

"You did?"

"You bet," Lila said with a snort of satisfaction. "I think he's a *snake*. Why, I'd as soon as marry smelly old Walt Forney, Grants's town drunk, as marry John Jacob."

"That's pretty strong talk," Ned called out from behind them.

"I mean it," Lila assured them both. "And for the life of me I can't understand why John keeps trying to get me to change my mind about him."

"Look in the mirror and you'll figure it out," Ned told her.

"Thank you," Lila called back to the newspaperman. "I'll take that as a compliment."

"That's the way it was intended."

Longarm was fuming. Ned Corey, it was beginning to appear, was smitten with Lila, and that was most likely going to become a meddlesome problem.

The KC Ranch wasn't more than a few hours' ride north of Grants. The ranch property was on a bit higher ground and surrounded by beautiful, high, vermilion-colored bluffs. It was fine-looking country, and although Longarm wasn't a rancher, he could see that the land was covered with good grass, and he observed plenty of fat deer and antelope. They crossed over several streams, and the nearer they got to the Chandler family's KC Ranch, the more Longarm could understand why John Jacob really wanted to own it.

"How many acres come with your ranch?" he asked.

"Four sections."

Longarm did a quick calculation. "That's just over twenty-five hundred acres."

"Yep," Lila said. "Twenty-five hundred and sixty, to be exact. And all of it is good grassy meadow and bottomland. Grama grass mostly, which is excellent feed for the cattle . . . if we still owned any. I talked my father into keeping our best bull and a couple of cows and heifers. I hope he hasn't sold even those off while I've been gone."

"He hasn't," Longarm said, pointing. "That must be them grazing out by that low hillock."

Lila brightened at the sight of their few remaining KC Ranch cattle and some horses as well. "Those are ours, all right! And we'll need to catch the horses up tomorrow for our trip to town and then use them to get to Skull Mountain. That short, stocky blue roan is mine. I named him Blueberry."

"What about me?" Ned called up to them.

Lila glanced at him. "Can you ride a horse, newspaperman?"

"Yeah, but not well."

"Then I'll put you on the chestnut gelding we call Beaver. He's slow but steady."

"Which one will I be riding?" Longarm asked.

"That palomino. He's a big, fast gelding and you'll like him. He was the last horse my father used to ride when he was chasing outlaws. We call him Sunny. The other two horses are the ones that we'll use as our pack animals when we leave for Skull Mountain."

Longarm saw the modest log-sided ranch house about a quarter mile up ahead. There was also a barn, a windmill, and holding pens for the cattle; everything was surrounded by huge cottonwood trees whose leaves looked silver-gray in the bright sunlight.

"Yeah," Lila said, as if reading his mind. "The house isn't much, but it's home to me and my folks, and has been for over ten years. When my parents bought the land, the cabin and the barn were standing, but we've added most of the cattle pens and horse corrals. Planted some trees. Dug a deeper well, erected the windmill, and made a lot of small and inexpensive improvements. In the summertime, it's nice to have all the shade we get from the cottonwoods, and they also form a pretty good windbreak.

"It's a beautiful place and the ranchland you own is impressive," Longarm told her. "Anyone would love to own the KC Ranch."

"That's what John Jacob thinks, too. He told me that once when he'd had a few too many drinks. John knows that we have the best water in the whole area, and he says that whoever has the best water has the best land. For once, I think that banker is right."

"I can't imagine a man like Jacob living this far out of town. He just doesn't seem to be the sort," Ned commented.

"Oh, he isn't," Lila answered. "But he still wants our ranch, and if we don't find that gold on Skull Mountain, I'm afraid he'll soon have it."

"Then we just *have* to find Joshua Bixby's gold," Ned said with determination in his voice. "We'll keep looking until we find it, and we won't give up."

"I like your spirit, Ned." She looked sideways at Longarm. "Don't you just love Ned's spirit?"

"Sure do," Longarm said without a hint of enthusiasm.

As Longarm drove the wagon into the yard, he was struck by the fact that no one came out of the ranch house to greet them. An old yellow hound dog did come around from the back the cabin to give a few fitful barks, but otherwise, all was silent in the yard.

"Something is *very* wrong," Lila said, her eyes darting back and forth across the front porch. "Father and Mother ought to be out here to greet us."

Longarm pulled up on the lines and the old horse was grateful to come to a stop and lower its big head.

Lila jumped down from the buckboard. "Dad! Mom! I'm home!"

Still no sound or sight of anyone.

Lila ran up to her door and tore it open while Longarm and Ned climbed down from the wagon and stood out in the yard, not sure of what to do.

Lila burst into the cabin and a moment later, they heard her scream, "Oh no!"

Longarm bolted toward the door and rushed inside to see Lila standing with her hand over her mouth. Longarm followed her gaze to the old man sitting in a rocking chair with a bullet hole in his chest and a clenched pistol resting in his lap.

Longarm went up to the man, already knowing he was dead and that this was the legendary Kenyon Chandler. "Lila, he's long gone. I'm sorry."

"My father . . . shot himself?"

"I'm afraid so."

She broke down in tears and staggered into a bedroom. "Where's Mother!"

The next few minutes were chaotic, and it was Ned Corey who found the fresh grave out behind the house and the simple wooden cross that had been carved to read: *Mrs. Chandler R.I.P.*

They all stood beside the grave and it was easy to see that it was fresh.

"I wish you both could have known them," Lila said, tears streaming down her cheeks. "They were fine, fine people."

"I'm sorry," Ned told her. "I wish I could have known them, too."

"Same here," Longarm told the grieving young cowgirl.

"I guess Father didn't see any point in living anymore with Mother gone."

"I guess not," Longarm said. "I'll find a shovel. We'll bury your father right here beside your mother, and I'll make him a cross to match your mother's."

"It's strange that Father didn't carve in Mother's first name, Mildred," Lila said wiping tears from her eyes. "And her birth and death dates."

"Your father was in poor health and maybe he just didn't have the strength."

"Yeah, I guess that's the reason," Lila said, walking away crying.

Longarm and Ned dug a deep grave for the old lawman, but when they went to lift him out of the chair, Longarm froze.

"What?" Ned asked.

"The back of his head has a spot that's crusted with dried blood."

Ned gently parted the old man's long hair. "Mr. Chandler must have hit his head pretty hard on something before he shot himself. No sense in pointing it out to Lila."

Longarm had seen a lot of head injuries in his life, most of them during his dangerous years as a lawman. And most of the ones he'd seen had not been accidental head injuries, but instead the result of men fighting and busting things over each other's skulls. He'd also perfected the art of pistol-whipping drunks and others who refused to be arrested, figuring that a well-administered pistol-whipping was a lot easier on a man than being shot.

"Kenyon was *pistol-whipped*," Longarm told the newspaperman. "Someone struck him across the back of his head hard enough to knock him out cold, maybe even kill him."

"Are you sure?"

Longarm nodded. "Yes. And it would also explain the cross that he carved over his wife's grave."

"You mean the fact that he called her Mrs. Chandler?"

"Yeah."

"That did seem strange and impersonal."

"I thought so, too," Longarm told the man. "And carving her birth date on that simple wooden cross would also have been impossible for a killer because he'd have no way of knowing it."

"Custis, you're right!"

"It's all starting to fall into place," Longarm said, removing the six-gun from Kenyon's stiff fingers. He sniffed at the barrel and found five rounds in the cylinder. It was now his professional opinion that Kenyon

Chandler's pistol had not been fired in weeks if not months. The other thing was that most old-time lawmen and a lot of new ones only carried five beans in their revolvers. Longarm was willing to bet that old Kenyon Chandler had been one of them.

"Are you quite certain this is murder?" Ned asked, voice low and strained so that Lila could not overhear them from the kitchen where she was making coffee.

"Everything I see is telling me that Lila's father was pistol-whipped, shot, and then put into this rocking chair so that it looked like he had committed suicide."

"But . . ."

"There's only one way to be sure," Longarm interrupted, looking deep into the younger man's eyes.

"No!" Ned protested, backing away with a look of horror on his face. "You want to dig up Lila's mother to see if she was also murdered?"

"Can you think of any other way to make sure that we have a murderer at work?" Longarm asked coldly.

Ned stepped out on the porch and stared off into the distance for a full minute before he turned to Longarm. "Don't you understand that if someone really did murder her parents, it will be twice as hard on Lila?"

Longarm expelled a deep breath, "Yeah, Ned, I've already thought of that. But let me ask you a question."

"Go on."

"If you were Lila, wouldn't you want to know the *truth*? And wouldn't you feel better learning that your father was murdered than that he was so despondent that he shot himself to death?"

After a long pause for deliberation, Ned reluctantly dipped his chin in agreement. "Yes to both questions."

"I'll talk to Lila," Longarm said quietly.

He went into the kitchen and, with as few words as possible, told the young ranch woman that he thought her father had been pistol-whipped and then murdered, and that, if that were true, then there was a very strong possibility that her mother had also been murdered.

Lila grabbed Longarm and clung to him for support. He felt her sobbing in his arms and he almost wished that he had not seen the injury on the back of the old lawman's head and reached his chilling conclusion.

"So, if you're right and my father was struck down, then put in the chair and shot, what . . . ?"

"That's just my *theory*," Longarm said. "And there's only one way that I can think of to prove if it's right or wrong."

"That being?"

"Your mother," Longarm said softly. "She hasn't been in that grave very long, and . . ."

"No!" Lila cried, breaking away from his arms. "Custis, that's terrible. You can't dig her up!"

"All right," he said, raising his hands. "We won't."

Longarm turned and walked out of the kitchen. "Ned, let's get Mr. Chandler out of that chair and . . ."

But Lila cut off his words as she followed on his heels. "Custis," she whispered, voice strained with grief. "Is that the *only* way you can prove if my father and mother were murdered?"

"It's the only way that I can think of. Maybe you or Ned can think of an . . . an easier way to tell."

Ned and Lila both slowly shook their heads.

"Then what would you have me do?" Longarm asked the woman. "It's your call, not mine."

"Dig up my mother and see if she was murdered," Lila said in a voice that sounded strange to all of them.

"Okay," Longarm said, dreading the job that lay before him but at the same time desperate to learn the truth. "Okay."

Chapter 8

"Ned, I think it would be best if you stayed with Lila in the cabin," Longarm ordered. "If I'm right and her mother was murdered, this could be too hard on her to witness."

"All right," Ned said, not even bothering to hide his relief.

"Tell Lila that I'll come in and tell you what I've found as soon as I've examined and reburied her mother."

"I'll do that."

"Good," Longarm said, grabbing up a shovel he'd picked up in the barn.

When Ned went into the cabin, Longarm set right to work at the digging. The grave being fresh, the ground was soft, and he was careful not to go at it too vigorously because he did not want to damage the old woman's corpse. It was his opinion that if Mrs. Chandler really had been murdered, she would have been buried in haste and not very deep.

Ten minutes after he started, the blade of his shovel came up against the yielding flesh of a body. Longarm took a deep breath, wishing that he didn't have to do this, but he knew that there was no choice if the truth about the Chandlers' deaths was to be discovered. So, as carefully as possible, he shoveled away the dirt and then crouched and gently brushed the loose earth from the old woman's small, unwrapped body. She was dressed in nothing but a tattered nightgown.

"Damn!" he hissed, recoiling.

Longarm rocked back on his heels and stared at the ugly bullet hole in Mildred Chandler's forehead. "A forty-five slug hit her almost right between the eyes."

He didn't have to raise Mildred Chandler's head to know that the bullet had also blown out the back of her skull. And since there was no blood in the house other than what had been under the rocking chair, it was obvious that whoever had shot the poor woman had done it out in the yard and then easily carried her over here to then dig this shallow grave.

"We'll find out who did this to you and your husband," Longarm whispered as he eased the woman's body back into her grave and then covered her up again. Because the grave was shallow, allowing the corpse to be violated by predators, he and Ned would need to cover it with rocks or a high mound of dirt tomorrow.

Longarm dreaded seeing Lila again and telling her what he'd discovered, but there was no choice in the matter. The moment he entered the cabin, he said, "There's no doubt that your mother was murdered."

It almost broke Longarm's heart to watch Lila struggle to retain her composure. To get her mind off what must have been terribly dark thoughts, he added, "There's still some daylight left, Ned. We ought to go out and look for fresh tracks other than our own."

Ned blinked. "That's a fine idea."

"All right," Lila said distantly.

"No," Longarm told her. "It would help more if you went into your parents' bedroom and checked to see if anything is missing. Anything valuable that you know your father kept in the bedroom or out here in the front room."

She nodded her head in vague agreement and Longarm grabbed Ned by the arm and dragged him outside. "Stick just a little behind me. I'm going to start out circling the yard and cabin. What we're looking for are the tracks of horses."

"How would you know they weren't those KC Ranch horses we saw grazing on our way in?"

"These horses will likely be leaving a heavy imprint and they'll almost surely be shod," Longarm told the man. "Also, look for anything else that I could miss."

"Like what, for instance?"

"A cigarette butt. A burnt match. The deep imprint of a boot heel where it wouldn't normally be found. Anything at all. Four eyes are better than two in this work."

"Okay."

Longarm was being only half truthful. The fact was that he had proven himself to be an excellent tracker around a crime scene. He had a practiced eye and knew what to look for, although he was admittedly less competent than a professional Indian tracker like the Army preferred to use.

So they began a small circle around the ranch yard. Unfortunately, a summer rain had fallen the day before, which made things more difficult. But Longarm did not think it had been a hard rain and he felt confident that any deep tracks would remain. Also, anything left behind by the killer or killers was going to be a sure tip-off.

"Lila is taking this pretty well, I think," Ned was saying as they began their second and wider circle around the ranch yard. "A lot of women would have gone into hysterics."

"That's true," Longarm said, his eyes straining as the light had began to fade. "Lila is strong, and maybe it helps that she knew her parents were both in failing health."

"I'm not sure that would matter," Ned told him. "What I can't understand is why anyone would murder Mr. and Mrs. Chandler and make it look like a suicide."

"Could be a lot of reasons, Ned. These are hard times, and there are bound to be men just roaming around looking for work, for a horse to steal, a cow to butcher, or an old man in failing health and a dying woman. And if you murdered Kenyon and Mildred Chandler, why not take just a little extra time and make it look like the old lawman committed suicide? By doing that, you'd eliminate the threat of getting caught."

"But Kenyon Chandler wouldn't have been an easy

victim, because from what I've heard, he was a very dangerous man."

"Kenyon was in very poor health with a festering bullet wound in his side. I wouldn't be surprised if he was also hard of hearing," Longarm explained. "No disrespect to the man, because he was a legend, but at his age, Kenyon Chandler was probably easy pickings."

"What kind of a person would take advantage of two old people in poor health?"

"There are men who would do it for a gawdamn dollar," Longarm said, his voice hardening with anger. "I've seen them, killed them, and sent them to the gallows many a time."

"What the hell are things coming to these days?"

"It's always been this way," Longarm said, abruptly stopping and reaching down to finger what appeared to him to be the mark of a boot heel.

"You find something?" Ned asked.

"Maybe."

"Look," Ned said, rushing forward to bend and reach into the grass. "Just like you said, a cigarette butt!"

"Then we've found our killer," Longarm said, nodding with satisfaction. He looked up ahead and said, "I'd wager we find where he tied his horse out of sight in that stand of cottonwoods."

"You think so?"

"I'd be willing to bet on it," Longarm answered, hurrying forward.

Sure enough, in the cottonwoods that stood about thirty yards south of the cabin there were plainly visible marks indicating where a nervous horse had stood for a short while.

"Custis, how do you read this?" Ned asked, unable to hide his excitement.

Longarm crouched and fingered the hoofprints and then the boot prints only partially lost to the rain. "The man wasn't big," he said. "His prints are smaller than you'd make. No rowel marks, so he didn't wear spurs, and his boots were round-toed and low-heeled. His horse was shod, as I'd expected. It toed in on the fronts and had small hooves. One horseshoe is fresher than the others."

"How can you tell?" Ned asked, leaning closer to stare hard at the prints.

"Because one shoe still has visible nail heads. It was probably nailed on in just the past few days and there wasn't time for it to wear smooth like the other three badly worn shoes."

"That's impressive," Ned told him.

"I've been at this awhile."

"Anything else?"

Longarm stood and walked all around where the horse had been tied to the cottonwood tree. "Afraid not," he said at last.

Ned's face fell. "Then that's not all too helpful, is it?"

"It narrows things down a mite." Longarm walked off a ways and raised his arm to point. "The killer left here heading west at a fast gallop. I can tell that because the hoofprints cupped dirt, so I know his horse was running hard."

Ned tossed the wet cigarette butt aside, placed his hands on his hips, and asked, "So what are we going to do about him?"

"I'm going to think on it tonight," Longarm replied. "In the morning I'll follow those tracks, although our killer has a long head start."

"What about our gold hunting on Skull Mountain?"

Longarm shrugged his broad shoulders. "I can always meet you and Lila there after I've either caught up with the killer or lost his trail."

"I don't like the idea of not having you with us."

"I'm not too happy about it, either," Longarm assured the man. "But I won't be gone for more than a couple of days."

"Meaning that's how long it'll take for you to either catch him or lose him."

"That's right."

"Damn," Ned whispered, "this sure has turned out bad for Lila."

"She's strong in her mind and she'll get past it," Longarm said. "But here's the thing, Ned. You've got to watch over her real carefully. Can you handle a gun or a rifle?"

"I've never shot at anyone," Ned confessed. "But I have done some target practice."

" 'Target practice'?" Longarm asked, not bothering to hide his skepticism.

"That's right. And I overheard Lila telling you that she's a real good shot."

"If I don't overtake her parents' killer in the next day or two, I'll ride straight for Skull Mountain."

"Do you even know where it is?"

"No, but Lila can give me directions tonight."

They started back toward the cabin. "Custis, this whole thing is starting out real bad, isn't it," Ned mused. "Snake-bit from the start."

"Doesn't mean that it won't turn out all right."

"I know. But I'm just getting a bad feeling about everything."

Longarm stopped and turned on the man. "Ned, are you already thinking about quitting? You said you weren't going to do that."

"And I won't!"

"All right then," Longarm said. "Let's tell Lila what we've found and tomorrow we'll split up and get after business."

"Maybe tomorrow our luck will start to change."

Longarm glanced sideways at the newspaper man and wondered if young Ned Corey would be any damn good at all if things went to hell up on Skull Mountain.

Chapter 9

Deep into the night, Lila and Longarm lay entwined in each other's arms, listening to the crickets outside and the distant howl of a coyote.

"It's been a hell of a homecoming," Longarm said quietly. "I'm sorry for what happened to your parents."

"Me, too. It helps a little that I'm sure Mother didn't have much longer to live. But Father might have lasted another year or two. And I really wanted you to meet and get to know them."

Lila turned to Longarm in the faint moonlight cast through their open window. There were fresh tears on her cheeks. "Custis, who on earth could have done this terrible thing to my folks? And why?"

He had been asking the same question to himself over and over. "I'm thinking that it could be someone who held an old grudge against your father. Someone Marshal Kenyon Chandler sent to prison or the gallows, or even the son or brother of that condemned man. Lila, when you're a lawman for as long as your father was, there are probably dozens of people who hold a lifelong grudge against you. Men who will fester inside while waiting and scheming for years to get what they've come to believe is their just revenge."

"Custis, are there such people right now waiting to get their revenge against you?"

"I'm sure that there are," Longarm replied. "It's something that always comes with our job as lawmen. I've never understood how evil, vile criminals manage to convince themselves that nothing they ever did was wrong or their own fault. They always create some powerful excuse to justify their cruel injustices. And when they go to prison, they meet other twisted and bitter men who feel exactly the same way and support them in their hatred and self-justified need for revenge."

Lila was silent for a few minutes and then said, "Do you think that the person who did this has any connection to John Jacob?"

"You mean that fancy banker?"

"Yes. He wants this place so badly. And he wants me in the bargain."

Longarm considered her blunt question. "It's not impossible that there's a connection between the murders and the banker. But why would banker Jacob have your parents murdered if all he had to do was just sit back and wait for his bank to foreclose?"

"Maybe he thought I was going to be successful getting help in Denver. And maybe he thinks that, with my parents murdered, I'll emotionally fall apart and rush to the comfort of his arms."

"Maybe," Longarm said. "Or the killer simply could have been a drifter or one of those longtime enemies I spoke of earlier who was seeking his revenge. Lila, did you find anything missing in this house?"

"As a matter of fact, I did. My father had a beautiful Winchester rifle that was given to him by the former territorial governor. It had silver inlaid in the front and back of the stock."

"Was the silver inscribed with your father's name?"

"No. But it was very unusual and you'd recognize it in a minute if you saw it. My father kept the rifle over the mantel and he was so proud of it that he'd only shoot that Winchester when someone who really appreciated firearms was present to watch and admire the weapon. He also had a pair of silver spurs to match, and they were given to him by the president of the Santa Fe Railroad for catching a train robber and returning the stolen money. The spurs *did* have his KC initials, but they were on the insides of the spurs where they couldn't be seen and didn't detract from the silversmith's ornate design."

"And you're sure that the spurs are also missing?"

"Absolutely. When my father got older and his back was stiff, it became harder and harder for him to bend over and buckle on the spurs. At my suggestion, he kept them cinched around a pair of custom-made black boots, which he always kept polished to a shine. The black boots and the spurs are both missing."

"Then if the man who killed your parents is still

alive," Longarm mused, "and if he's wearing the boots and spurs, he ought to be plenty easy for me to pick out of a crowd."

"Where will you go looking?"

"I'll follow the tracks to wherever they lead," Longarm told her. "From what I could tell, they were headed straight west."

"Toward the Navajo Reservation?"

"Yes, into the Arizona Territory. Maybe our man went only as far as Gallup, New Mexico, but he could have bought a train ticket and continued on to Holbrook, Winslow, or even Flagstaff, Arizona."

"I hope you don't have to chase those tracks clear into Arizona."

"Me, too," Longarm said. "I'll need your palomino and a packhorse. I'll bring them back."

"I know that."

"And you and Ned can go up on Skull Mountain and start hunting for that gold mine."

"Yes," Lila said. "But without you there . . . well . . . it won't be nearly the same for me."

"Meaning?"

"I'll miss you terribly," Lila said, hugging his neck and then kissing his mouth.

Longarm had expected that she would not want to make love, given the tragedy she'd faced earlier in the day, but he was wrong. Lila climbed up on him and her passion was greater than it had ever been in Denver. She took his manhood in her hands and worked it up and down until Longarm was big and stiff. Then, she bent down, took him into her mouth, and sucked on him until the pleasure was overpowering.

"Easy." He groaned. "Mount up and give yourself a hard ride, girl!"

Lila guided him into herself. Moments later, she reared up on her knees, arched her back, and began to pound up and down, pistoning his manhood into herself and using him like a bucking horse.

Longarm laughed and let her seek all the pleasure she could find. When she threw her head back and cried out in ecstasy, he rolled Lila onto her back and went at her with a savage delight. Moments later he erupted, and torrents of his seed filled the New Mexico cowgirl. He whooped so loud that even the coyote stopped howling out in the night.

"Good heavens!" Lila said after a few minutes when they'd both caught their breath. "If townsfolk were listening, they would have heard us both all the way into Grants."

"And you can bet that Ned Corey sure heard us from the next room."

"Yes, I'm sure that he did." Lila kissed Longarm's rugged face. "But I don't care. This is my house now and I want Ned to understand that you are *my* man."

"He won't have any doubts about that point after hearing us just now." Longarm chuckled.

"No," she said, wrapping one of her long legs over his, "I'm sure he won't."

"Lila?"

"Yes?"

"Go well armed to Skull Mountain," Longarm cautioned. "Ned tells me that he can shoot reasonably well, but don't count on him."

"We'll be all right."

"You need to tell me exactly where Skull Mountain is so that I can ride straight for it after I bring your parents' killer to justice."

"While you and Ned were outside, I drew you a map relative to Grants. Skull Mountain is big, and you won't have any trouble finding it. Just hunt down the sonofabitch who killed Mother and Father and *kill* him."

"I'm a lawman, not a hired gun or executioner," Longarm told her. "But don't worry, when I find the killer, if I don't have to shoot him dead, I'll make damn sure that he hangs."

"I wish I could be there to watch him dance his way into hell," she said passionately.

"Maybe you really don't," Longarm told her. "I've seen plenty of hangings, and no matter how much they were deserved, it was never anything but a sad and sickening spectacle. Some people come from miles around to watch a hanging, but I've never understood their sick fascination. Lila, the memory of a body's last violent kicking and choking moments will forever sear your mind. Some people who have come to watch and maybe even smiled at the time later told me that they'd had nightmares of a body in its final agonizing death throes."

"The man who killed my parents *deserves* to die in agony," Lila said. "I just hope that he killed my father before he got to Mother."

Longarm understood her meaning. A man like Kenyon Chandler would have died a hundred deaths if he had been forced to watch his wife being executed while he'd been unable to save her.

"Let's go to sleep," Longarm suggested. "We're both going to have tough days ahead."

"I hope it doesn't rain any more and wipe out the last of the man's tracks."

"If it does, then I'll ride into Gallup and see if anyone has seen a stranger with silver spurs and silver inlay in the stock of a Winchester rifle. Those are things that will attract attention and be remembered."

"Ned and I will be leaving at the same time you do to head for Grants to buy some supplies. I might stop and pay a visit to the bank just to see if John Jacob can look me squarely in the eye. And if he can't do that, then I'll know that he had a part in these murders."

"I'd rather you stayed away from him," Longarm told her. "When I catch the man that shot your parents, I'm going to do everything in my power to take him alive. After that, I'll find out if he just happened to ride across the KC Ranch and then decided to kill your parents, or if he was hired to do it by banker Jacob."

"I see." Lila nodded at the ceiling. "Yes, if the killer confesses, I guess that would be the best thing."

"Let's sleep," Longarm said. "If we can."

Chapter 10

Because it took them a while to catch up the KC Ranch horses, Longarm knew that they weren't going to get all that early of a start. Even so, the eastern sun wasn't far over the broken vermilion cliffs when Longarm said, "Lila, I'll see you and Ned up on Skull Mountain in a few days, a week at the longest. Whatever you do, don't let anyone in Grants know that you're going off to hunt for gold."

"Of course not."

Lila gave him a good-bye hug and kiss while Ned Corey stood off to the side admiring the long line of the cliffs' brilliant and constantly changing colors. "This country is beautiful," he said to no one in particular. "I've never seen such stunning and impressive sandstone cliffs."

Longarm mounted his gelding and smiled. "So long, Ned."

"So long, Custis. We'll be looking for you on the mountain."

Longarm didn't glance back as he galloped out of the
ranch yard and picked up the tracks left by a murderer's
horse. He was guessing that whoever had killed Lila's
parents was not going to stray far from the westbound
Santa Fe Railroad. The man would not have found much
in the way of cash to steal in the KC Ranch home, but
the Winchester and spurs . . . now those would be worth
a lot of money, and Longarm was hoping the killer
needed quick cash. If he did, he'd try to sell his stolen
prizes in Gallup, or maybe in Holbrook or Winslow. He
wouldn't be likely to go up into the Navajo Reservation
because while those people would greatly covet a prized
rifle and silver spurs, they wouldn't have much cash and
they were very likely to take it from a lone white man by
using deadly force.

"I'm betting he's following the railroad towns until
he gets what he thinks is a fair price for that silver
inlaid rifle and pair of fancy spurs," he said aloud as the
palomino carried him swiftly across the broken country.

The palomino was a good riding horse, and Longarm
was enjoying his ride this morning. He watched a red-
tailed hawk circle up in the sky, waiting to sight a rabbit
or prairie dog. The country was much to his liking, with
plenty of grass and even some ancient Indian ruins high
up on the cliffs. Longarm had never seen Chaco Canyon,
but he'd heard about it and knew that it wasn't more than
fifty miles distant as the crow flies.

"Some other time," he said to himself, thinking about
how Kenyon Chandler and his wife had died. It was his

suspicion that someone must have tied his horse up in that small stand of cottonwoods, then sneaked into the house and shot Kenyon dead in his rocking chair. After that, he must have caught the old woman outside, perhaps sitting on the porch or out in the barn doing some chores, or maybe just watching the sun rise or set. Either way, they were both dead, and they sure as hell hadn't deserved such a bad ending. Longarm was just thankful that Lila hadn't been at the ranch. But then again, perhaps she would have killed the intruder and saved her parents.

But none of that mattered anymore. The only good thing about this whole situation was that Lila was alive and she seemed to be taking the death of her parents as well as could be expected. Lila said it helped that they had both been old and her mother in failing health, but it had to still be hard.

Far up ahead Longarm could see thunderheads building, and that wasn't a welcome sight. The tracks that he followed were plain enough, but in this country the vast empty sky could suddenly rain buckets, and these deep gullies and gorges that he was constantly crossing could fill with deadly flash floods.

About ten miles west of the KC Ranch the tracks began to angle toward distant Gallup and the railroad tracks. That was good news; the bad news was the skies were growing ever darker and Longarm could hear the approaching rumble of thunder. He was headed for a storm and that meant that he was out in this wild and desolate country exposed to lightning and foul weather. But even worse, he was going to lose the killer's tracks.

Lila and Ned rode into the railroad town of Grants at mid-morning, dragging two packhorses in their wake. The town was as busy as it ever got, with a few wagons transporting goods from one place to another and several people moving around to do their early business. To the east beside the rail lines, cowboys were raising a big cloud of dust in the cattle corrals, and Lila figured they were getting a small herd ready to ship on the train. As Lila and Ned rode past the Pinto Pony Hotel, Homer Monroe stepped out onto his porch with a broom in his chubby hands, sweeping dust into the street. When he saw Lila and Ned, he called, "Good morning!"

"Good morning."

"Come on in and have some breakfast!"

Ned said to Lila, "That does sound like a fine idea. My stomach is growling."

"Mine, too," Lila told him in a low voice as she angled her roan to the hotel's hitch rail. Since before dawn she'd been so focused on rounding up the saddle and packhorses that breakfast had not been a consideration. "Let's have a quick breakfast before we buy supplies and head out. But remember, no mention of Skull Mountain."

Ned appeared to be a little weary of this constant reminder. "Don't worry."

"When Homer asks, and he will, just say we are going up to take in the sights at Chaco Canyon. Tell him you're interested in ancient Indians and American West archaeology."

"I am, actually. You should see my collection of arrowheads and Anasazi pottery."

"That's good," Lila said as they tied their animals at the hitch rail and went inside with Monroe, who led them to his best table and said, "Sit down and I'll get some of my good coffee over here."

The owner called out to his kitchen staff and soon they had coffee and were settling in for ham, eggs, and potatoes all around. "Fine morning," Homer Monroe said, grinning, "but it looks to me like we've got a storm coming in from the west."

"We saw it, too," Lila told the man.

"Where's Marshal Custis Long? I didn't see him ride in with you just now."

"He had some things to do."

Homer Monroe's eyes narrowed with suspicion. "He had things to do at your ranch?"

"And he wasn't feeling so well this morning, so we told him just to rest easy."

"I hope it wasn't what he ate here in my restaurant."

"No," Lila assured the hotel owner. "He thoroughly enjoyed the meal he had here."

"That's a relief to hear. So what brings you to town with packhorses?"

"We're riding up to take a look at Chaco Canyon," Ned told the hotelman. "I've always wanted to see it, and even though it's a bit of a ride, now is our chance to do it."

"I've been up there a few times," Monroe told them. "The place is amazing! All those walls and crumbling adobe structures. And those great round ceremonial pits they're calling kivas. Why, there must have been a thousand people or more living at Chaco Canyon."

"I'd think so," Lila said.

Homer Monroe was getting enthused with the subject and the mystery. "And can you imagine! After going to all that work, all those ancient Indians just up and disappeared! Or maybe they were attacked and wiped out or taken off as slaves. What do you think, Lila?"

"I have no earthly idea," she replied. "All I'm sure of is that there must have been a lot of workers there for centuries to have built that massive city of stone and mortar."

"I have a theory that the Apache came and killed 'em all off," Monroe said.

"I doubt that is what caused those people to disappear," Ned replied.

Homer Monroe's fork stopped just short of his mouth. "Why not?"

"Because," Ned explained, "even though I've never been to Chaco Canyon, I've read about it and seen photographs. And, if I remember correctly, the first white men to discover the ancient city said that there were no skeletons, no bones or any signs that there had been a big fight or a massacre."

Monroe barked a laugh. "Well, hellfire, son! Bones ain't *stones*! Bones disintegrate over time. Remember that somewhere in the Bible it says 'ashes to ashes and dust to dust'?"

"Yeah, I remember, but the people who study old Indian ruins say that it's more likely that the water gave out in Chaco Canyon and the people had to move away in order to survive."

Homer Monroe shook his head. "I think that's dead wrong, son. You ask me, I'd say that the people that built all those ruins just worked themselves down to skin and bone and were easy pickin's for the Apache. The Apache are mean and murderous, and they probably chopped the heads off the males and took the females for their slaves and wives. I just always hoped they didn't wipe out the kids when they attacked and wiped out Chaco."

Lila sat back and listened to the two men argue the fate of a civilization that had lived around a thousand years ago, and ate her breakfast. It was clear that both Homer and Ned liked to argue and conjecture on things that they had no real knowledge about. But neither man got mad or upset with the other, and so the meal went quickly and the lively conversation was entertaining.

"Ned," Lila said, finishing off her plate and then draining her coffee, "let's go buy a few supplies and get back to the ranch."

"Sounds good," Ned told her.

"You folks come back real soon, and tell that big fella to do the same!"

"I will," Lila promised. "Thanks for the breakfast, Homer."

"Tell your father and mother hello for old Homer."

Lila had to swallow hard. "I'll do it."

* * *

After leaving the Pinto Pony Hotel, they went to the general store and bought flour, beans, coffee, some extra ammunition, and a few other things that they were going to need on Skull Mountain, all the while telling people that they were heading off to visit Chaco Canyon.

"Good morning!"

They turned to see John Jacob coming toward them with an easy smile on his handsome face. "Well, well," he said, as he came out to greet them. "It's sure nice to see you again so soon, Lila. Who's your young friend?"

"This is Mr. Ned Corey from Raton. We're going out to do a little exploring at Chaco Canyon."

"That ought to be interesting. But I'm afraid it looks like there's a storm brewing to the west and it's heading our way."

"Maybe we'll wait at the ranch until it passes," Lila told the banker.

Now the banker turned his attention from Lila to ask, "Ned, are you a longtime friend of the Chandler family?"

"Uh . . . not really."

Lila bit her tongue. Before leaving, Longarm had advised them not to say anything about her parents being murdered. And although Custis hadn't explained his reasoning, Lila was just as glad not to get into that conversation, especially with banker John Jacob.

"Well," Jacob said, "did you two meet in Denver?"

"On the train," Lila said. "Ned is paying us to take

him out to Chaco, and we can always use the money . . . as well you know."

"Sure you can!" Jacob said, giving them both an engaging smile. "Lila, I asked your father to come into my bank and talk about the mortgage, but I guess it just slipped his mind."

"I guess it did."

Jacob's smooth smile slipped and his voice took on weight. "You had better remind him that the note is due in full in a couple of weeks."

"I'm sure he knows that. Now," Lila said, not sure of how much more of this conversation she could stand, "if you'll excuse us, John, we had better be heading back to the ranch before that storm arrives."

"You going to be sightseeing at Chaco Canyon for very long?"

"A while," Ned told the man. "Ever been there?"

"Not me," Jacob told the newspaperman. "I'm far more concerned with the living than I am a bunch of dead Indians."

"Excuse us," Lila said, starting to walk around the man. "We have to be leaving now."

Jacob caught her by the arm. "You sure seem to be in a big hurry this morning, Lila. Where is that big fella that you came in with off the train?"

"You must be referring to Marshal Custis Long."

The banker's jaw dropped. "He's a *marshal*?"

Lila almost smiled because it was so comical to see the sudden alarm on John Jacob's handsome face. "That's right. A *federal* marshal from Denver."

"Don't tell me that he's also interested in seeing those old Indian ruins."

"As a matter of fact," Lila said, almost enjoying herself, "he is."

"I don't believe it!"

"It's true."

Jacob shook his head and clucked his tongue. "How odd that you go to Denver and come back with two men interested in Chaco Canyon."

"Yes, isn't it odd," Lila said, shaking loose of his grip and walking toward her horses.

"Say hello to your mother and father!" Jacob called. "Tell your father that I'll look forward to seeing him in the next day or two."

"I'll do that," Lila said tightly as she untied their horses and climbed onto Blueberry.

"And come by and visit me anytime, Lila! You can even bring your two male admirers!"

Lila didn't give the banker the courtesy of a reply as she and Ned hurried their horses up the street and out of Grants. As soon as they were out of sight of the little railroad town, Lila reined her horse to the northwest toward the KC Ranch and said, "I think everyone in town believed us about going off to explore the ruins in Chaco. Even that bastard, Jacob."

"You're a pretty convincing liar," Ned told her.

"I guess I am," Lila replied. "And you didn't do too badly yourself."

"I feel a bit guilty about it," Ned told her.

"Me, too, except for lying to John Jacob. Didn't you

get the impression that he thought something was pretty fishy?"

"I got the impression that he was damned jealous of Custis and myself. He's a pushy one, and real full of himself."

"Yes, he is," Lila replied. "John Jacob thinks that he walks on water and he lords it over those who have less than he does . . . which is most everyone in Grants."

"I can see why you don't like him. Do you think he's suspicious of what we said?"

"If he is," Lila replied, "then it's because he might know that my parents are dead. And if he does know, then that is something that Custis needs to find out."

Ned pulled up his horse and said, "You don't really think that Mr. Jacob had anything to do with the murder of your parents, do you?"

"I wouldn't put it past him."

Ned Corey shook his head. "He wasn't even carrying a gun."

"He was carrying a gun, all right," Lila said with assurance. "There was a derringer up his sleeve and a small pistol resting in his coat pocket. John Jacob is not only handsome and charming, he's as deadly as a viper."

"I have the feeling that the banker smells something is amiss," Ned told her. "I am not sure that Mr. Jacob believed a thing that we told him. And the bad thing about the lying is that, the next time we go to Grants, we're going to have to make up a bunch more lies about how much we enjoyed Chaco."

"We'll do whatever we have to."

"That's the worst part about telling lies," Ned told her. "One lie just naturally leads to the next and the next. A lie is like an avalanche. It just snowballs and gets bigger and bigger until there is no stopping it."

"Maybe we'll visit Chaco Canyon if we have the time just so we can honestly say that we really went there."

"That's not a bad idea," Ned replied. "I really have always wanted to see it, but our main focus has to be on finding old Joshua Bixby's gold mine."

"I know," Lila said. "More than anything else in this world, I want to save my ranch."

"Are we going to stop by the ranch and wait out the storm?" Ned asked. "It's getting closer and louder by the minute."

"I think we'd better do that," Lila told him. "The ranch is not really much out of the way."

"I'm glad to hear you say that," Ned told her. "The idea of weathering a New Mexico storm isn't appealing."

"I know what you mean," Lila said. "I hope that Custis finds shelter before he gets hit with it."

"He's riding west, and that's where it's coming from."

"He could be almost to Gallup by now," Lila said. "And I hope he is."

"Don't worry about Marshal Custis Long," Ned told her. "If I ever met a man who could take care of most anything that came his way, then it's him."

"You're right," Lila said. "Let's put these horses into a

quick trot and get to the ranch before we get hammered by wind and rain."

"I'm all for that!" Ned called, bouncing up and down as the rough-gaited Beaver hammered his ass against the saddle.

Chapter 11

Longarm lost the tracks he was following about five miles northeast of Gallup, New Mexico, when the rain began to come down in a torrent. He pulled his flat-brimmed hat low, kicked the palomino into a trot, and dragged his packhorse into the railroad town feeling cold, wet, and miserable.

The only good thing that came to his mind as he rode right through an open livery barn door was that he was pretty sure that the man who had killed the Chandler couple had also taken refuge in Gallup. If he was lucky . . . real lucky . . . he might even find the horse he'd been tracking right here in this leaky old barn.

"Hello!" Longarm called, dismounting.

"Hello, yourself!" a voice called back moments before a man in bib overalls, heavy work boots, and a battered straw hat appeared smoking a corncob pipe. "What the hell you doin' out there in this kinda weather, mister?"

"Just trying to get here," Longarm told him.

The stableman was short and dirty, and in his late fifties. Longarm sized him up as being friendly and pretty eager for conversation. "My name is Custis and I'd like to put up these two horses tonight."

The man stuck out a calloused hand. "I'm Alvin P. Cornwell, and I own this barn and stable. It'll cost you two bits for each animal, but I feed and grain heavy, and I'll put 'em both under a spot where my roof ain't leakin' too badly."

"That's fair enough," Longarm said. "You have any other horses being boarded?"

Alvin's grin slipped and his eyes narrowed. "Why you asking?"

Longarm decided to play it straight with the liveryman, so he peeled back his coat to reveal his federal officer's badge. "I'm a United States Marshal and I'm looking for someone who's riding a horse that toes in on the front feet and has one shoe newer than the other three. This horse has small hooves."

"Marshal, I don't have such a horse being kept here," Alvin said without hesitation.

"Are you sure?"

"Hell yes! But you can see what's here for yourself." Alvin tamped the foul-smelling tobacco in his pipe and made a sweeping gesture with his left hand. "I'm only boarding three horses right now that are owned by out of towners."

"Maybe the man I'm after isn't an 'out of towner,'"

Longarm suggested. "Maybe he lives here in Gallup."

"Take a look at what I've got, Marshal."

"I'll do that," Longarm said, handing the reins of the palomino to the man and then the lead rope attached to his packhorse.

"You come a far piece?"

"From Denver."

Alvin's bushy eyebrows shot up. "Ridin' these two horses?"

"No. I came out to New Mexico on the train."

"Then where'd you get these horses?"

"It doesn't matter," Longarm said. "For a stable owner, you ask a lot of questions."

Alvin stuck his jaw out. "You started askin' 'em *first*."

"Yeah," Longarm admitted, "I guess I did at that."

Longarm took a quick look at each of the boarded horses and knew right away that none of them belonged to the killer he'd tracked from the KC Ranch.

"Sorry to disappoint you, Marshal."

"Are there any other stables here in Gallup?"

"Two others, but they're owned by dishonest men."

"I'll look in on them later," Longarm said. "Right now, I need to get dry, and I'm half starved."

"I'd recommend the Cattleman's Café, just a block up the street. That's where I eat most of the time."

"Thanks. What about a hotel?"

"You want cheap . . . or clean?"

"Clean," Longarm told the man.

"Then that would be the Frontier Hotel. It's located

just up the street past the Cattleman's Café. Tell Mrs.
Fetter that I sent you and she'll give you a good room
and a smile."

"I'll do that."

"Mrs. Fetter is older than dirt, but you might get
lucky and meet her daughter at the hotel's registration
desk. Her name is Hanna and she's damned frisky." Alvin winked. "For a dollar, she'll come up to your room
and make you think you are a mighty, mighty man."

"Is that right?"

"Sure is! She's worth the dollar, I can testify to that."
Alvin giggled childishly. "You see her and you'll want
her, if you don't mind your women with a little bounce
in their butts and lard on their legs."

"I don't need any complications."

"Hanna is the kind of complication that a man likes.
If I had more money than horse shit, I'd spend a dollar
every damn day for the rest of my life on Hanna. She's a
little on the tubby side, but she sure knows how to . . ."

"Thanks," Longarm said, cutting the man off, "but
I'm here on business, not pleasure."

"You after the person who rides that horse you're
lookin' for?"

"That's right."

"Tell me what the jasper looks like and maybe I can
tell you I saw him in Gallup."

"I don't know what he looks like," Longarm confessed.

"That does make it harder," Alvin said. "What's this
man done wrong?"

"I'd rather not say."

"Pretty bad stuff, huh?"

"Pretty bad," Longarm replied.

"He murder some poor fella?"

Longarm just smiled and left because he judged Alvin was not only curious, he was a gadfly and a gossip. The kind of good-hearted and gregarious man who would blab about a newly arrived marshal from Denver and a hunted killer that might be on the loose in Gallup, New Mexico. And unless Longarm was greatly mistaken, Alvin would soon be hurrying out of his barn to the nearest saloon and telling everyone damn near everything he'd learned in their brief and just concluded conversation.

The rain was coming down in buckets when he left the Cattleman's Café feeling a whole lot better for the steak and potatoes he'd consumed. The food had been excellent and the price fair. Longarm figured he'd have breakfast there in the morning and then he'd probably be leaving Gallup if the weather improved.

The Frontier Hotel was small but a man could see that it was well kept and clean. The tile floor of the lobby was waxed to a shine and there were even some potted plants to brighten the room. Longarm strode through the lobby, dripping water from his coat and hat and tracking some mud on the polished red tiles.

"Sorry about the mess," he said to the humpbacked old woman wearing dangling earrings and a red shawl around her shoulders, who now eyed him with disapproval. "It's pretty bad outside today."

"I ain't blind and I can see that, mister. But it wouldn't have hurt you none to have wiped your muddy boots on my front doormat and then shook the water off that funny-looking Stetson."

"Sorry," he said, deciding that old age and rheumatism from the wet, cold weather was the cause of her present foul disposition. "Alvin P. Cornwell told me that you ran a clean hotel and I can see that he was correct."

"It *was* clean until you tracked mud and rainwater across the floor."

Longarm bit back his irritation and asked, "Do you have a room I can rent for the night?"

"Sure do." The old crone glared at him. "What other reason would cause me to be standing in pain behind this registration desk looking up at your mug?"

"None, I guess. How much for the night?"

"Two dollars, and that includes a hot bath, soap, and a clean towel."

"Fair enough." Longarm dug two dollars from his wallet and laid them on the desk. "They're wet, but they'll spend as good as dry ones."

"I expect so," she said, her little hands like claws snapping up the money. Mrs. Fetter turned the registration book around for him to sign. "You sign this and I'll give you room six upstairs. Here's the key."

Longarm took the key and signed. The old woman was already knocking around in a back room and when she emerged, he saw that she had a mop in her bony, arthritic fists. "Next time I'll wipe my feet at the door, Mrs. Fetter."

"Be the civilized thing to do," she snapped as she went to mop up his muddy footprints. "People just don't seem to have any good sense or proper manners anymore."

Longarm decided to just keep his mouth shut and go upstairs. He was soaked and shivering. He'd take a hot bath, change into some at least partially dry clothes out of his canvas bag, and then go out to visit the saloons and perhaps those other two livery stables if it wasn't raining too hard. If he was in luck, he'd have his man arrested for murder before midnight.

Three hours later, Longarm returned to the Frontier Hotel again, wet and out of sorts. He wiped his boots off on the doormat and slapped the rain from his coat and hat before he entered the hotel.

His outing had been a huge disappointment. He'd visited the five saloons in Gallup and slipped the bartenders at each establishment a dollar, hoping for information, but to no avail. Tomorrow he'd slog through mud and check out the two other stables, but he wasn't at all optimistic about finding the horse he'd tracked almost to Gallup. Right now it seemed like the trail he'd followed from the KC Ranch had run ice-cold.

The crotchety old woman at the hotel desk was gone and in her place was a big, buxom blonde woman with a wide smile and bold eyes.

"Well, hello there, handsome!" She studied the registration book. "You would be Custis Long, the marshal from Denver."

Longarm had not written down in the registration book that he was from Denver or that he was a lawman. That meant that Alvin had been here and told this woman about his business.

"Yeah, I'm from Denver."

She was in her late twenties; her cheeks were rosy and her lips the color of blood. Leaning over across the desk, she showed a lot of cleavage and she let Longarm have his look before she straightened and said, "You find your wanted man out there?"

"Nope."

"Must be hard to find someone that you don't even know what he looks like."

Longarm had no intention of telling Hanna that he would know his killer if he saw him leaving town on a pigeon-toed horse with one shoe different from the other three.

"It's never easy," he said, faking a yawn. "But a real lawman doesn't give up the chase."

"You look like the kind of man who has had more than his share of chases. You ever chase wild women?"

"No," Longarm said. "They chase *me*."

It was the truth, but not at all modest, and Longarm was surprised he'd spoken those words. But he didn't retract them. "I'll say good night to you, miss."

"Hanna. I'm really the *owner* of this hotel. My mother thinks she's the owner, but she's not. I got a friendly local lawyer to make sure of that much. Anyway, I just humor her in her old age."

"She needs some humoring," Longarm said dryly.

"I got the impression that your mother isn't a happy person."

"She feels terrible in the joints when it's cold or rainy, but only miserable when the weather is fine. Did you have a bath already, Custis?"

"I'm going to do that right now," he said.

"Our Chinaman is gone for the night, but I'll bring you up some hot water, soap, and towels."

"Thanks."

"You're welcome."

Longarm went upstairs to his room and again removed his soggy coat, hat, and shirt. He sure hoped that this storm would soon pass. He had seen the bathroom at the end of the hall and now he walked barefooted down the hallway wearing only a damp undershirt and pants. As always, he kept his pistol, cartridge belt, and holster, because he never knew who he might run into that was having a bad time or that he'd offended or arrested in the past.

The bathroom was small, and as soon as he arrived, Hanna came in with a bucket of hot water in each hand and he could see that she was as broad as a horse across her back and ass end; no doubt Hanna Fetter was every bit as strong as a big Missouri mule.

"Don't just stand there, Marshal," she said, "shuck off those pants and climb in. I'll pour the bath water right over the top of you. It's hot, but not scalding. A bar of good soap is already in the tub."

Longarm was a little put off by her boldness, and he was not at all in the habit of undressing before a clothed woman. "Leave the buckets on the floor and I'll pour them over myself, thank you."

"What's the matter with you?" she asked. "You too modest to stand naked before me?"

"No."

"Then what? You got an itty bitty pecker?"

"Jaysus!" Longarm stormed. "Hanna, just . . . just get on out of here."

"You are a strange man, Marshal Long. And I should be deeply offended by your words, but I'll forgive you."

Hanna set the big buckets of hot water down beside the tub saying, "You need more water, just bang on the door twice and I'll bring you more."

"Okay."

"Good night, Marshal."

"Good night."

The door closed and Longarm had his bath. He took his time soaking, and the water was nearly cool when he stepped out of the tub and dried himself off. He now felt clean and refreshed and plenty ready for a good night's sleep. In the morning, he'd visit those two other stables. If it was still raining hard, he'd have to spend another night in his rented room and he'd insist on a second bath, since it came with the higher-than-average room rate.

Longarm went to bed hearing the storm beating against the roof and the window. He thought about Lila and Ned Corey and hoped that they were not stuck out in the country tonight. If they were, maybe they'd try to make it to Chaco Canyon and hole up in some ancient Indian ruins just to keep warm and dry. Longarm knew that he was pretty fortunate just to have made it to a clean Gallup hotel, and he sure hoped his luck would change for the better in the morning and he'd be able to find the man who had savagely murdered Kenyon Chandler and his poor, defenseless wife. Any sonofabitch that would do such a despicable and brutal act to a pair of nice folks did not deserve to breathe clean, fresh air.

.

Chapter 12

Sometime in the middle of that night while the wind still howled outside and the rain hammered the Frontier Hotel, Longarm heard the wooden floor of his room squeak under the pressure of a heavy weight. He rolled to his side, his hand snatching up his pistol. Cocking back the hammer, he yelled, "Freeze or you're dead!"

"Don't shoot me!"

"Hanna?"

"It ain't the fat tooth fairy."

Longarm uncocked his hammer and laid the pistol on his bedside table. "What on earth are you doing in my room in the middle of the night?"

"I got lonesome and hungry between my legs just thinking about *you*."

"Go away."

"Got a dollar, Custis? I'm not in the habit of doing it for free."

"I have a dollar, but I'm keeping it."

"You're a hard man, Marshal Long, but a damn good-looking one." Hanna came over to the bed and before Longarm quite knew what she was up to, she threw back the covers and climbed in beside him. The bed groaned under their combined weight and he suddenly realized she was as naked as the day she was born.

"Dammit, Hanna! I'm not interested in doing anything."

"I get real hungry for lovemaking on a cold and rainy night, Custis. I was thinking about you in my lonely bed and I started touching myself and getting excited."

"Oh for crying out loud. Hanna . . . Let go of me!"

"It ain't at all itty bitty." She giggled. "Just the opposite, in fact."

Longarm started to roll off the opposite side of the bed and get dressed, but Hanna was quicker and rolled on top of him, and that felt like being buried by a landslide. She threw her massive and meaty legs out to the edges of his bed, pinning him like a bug to a board.

"Now, I am gonna make you think that you are a real stud."

Hanna held his nuts in the palm of her big fist and when Longarm started to protest, she squeezed him hard enough to make him gasp and grow still.

"Now you just don't move and let little Miss Hanna take care of you."

Little Miss Hanna?

Hanna slid down his length and took Longarm's manhood in her mouth, then started sucking on it like a stick of peppermint candy. He was still forming a protest in his mind when he suddenly realized that he was getting aroused and he'd be a fool to object to what she was doing to him so expertly.

"Liking it?" she purred.

"Yes," he admitted. "It feels mighty good."

She licked his rising root from the top to the bottom. "Of course it does, honey! I was going to do this to you in the bathtub, but you got all uppity. I almost decided you didn't deserve me."

Hating himself for his weakness, Longarm said, "Every man makes a mistake now and then, Hanna."

She worked Longarm like a cherry flavored lollipop for a while, and when he couldn't stand it any longer, Hanna rolled over on her back like a beached whale, and damned if Longarm didn't jump right on her and give it all she was worth. He pounded and poked and panted, and when Hanna somehow got those massive legs wrapped around his waist, Longarm knew he was there to stay until both of them had their full measure of carnal satisfaction.

Two hours later, feeling battered and beaten, Longarm rolled out from under Hanna, gasping for air and sweating like a winning racehorse.

"Enough," he croaked. "I've had all I can take."

Hanna said, "You're a fine specimen of a man, Custis. How'd you like to marry me?"

"What!" He jumped up from the bed. "Hanna, surely you're joking."

"Maybe I am right now, but maybe after a week or so

of nights like this I *wouldn't* be joking. You'd get me and the hotel in the marriage bargain. No more running around after outlaws or sleeping on the cold, hard ground or dodging bullets."

"But I like what I do."

"You'd like it better being a hotel owner and my ever-lovin' husband."

Longarm couldn't believe what he was hearing. But he knew that Hanna was about half serious, and he decided to humor the woman.

"Well," he said, "I'm flattered by the thought of marrying you, but I just don't reckon I could last a day alongside your crabby mother."

"Aw, she's all bark and no bite, darlin'."

"Maybe so," Longarm said, "but she's critical and damned difficult."

"She is that, but she probably won't last a whole lot longer. I give the old gal about six months to live. After that, she's a goner."

"What makes you think so?"

"She's got pains other than in her joints. The doctor says that she's got cancer in her guts."

"That would be a hard way to go, Hanna."

"She's a hard woman and she's lived a long time. Outlasted three husbands and I don't know how many lovers. Broke every man she ever screwed and left 'em cryin', bitter, and broke. Don't feel sorry for my mother, Custis. She's got a heart of stone."

"It's finally stopped raining," Longarm said, not wanting to carry on this line of conversation. "I'm going to go to the other two stables in town looking for the horse that I followed over from near Grants."

"What did the man you're hunting *really* do?"

"He murdered an old couple at their ranch house and he stole a pair of silver inlaid spurs and a Winchester rifle."

"What!"

Longarm repeated himself and Hanna said, "Custis, I've seen a man wearing a pair of silver spurs and carrying a fancy Winchester."

"When?"

"Day before yesterday."

"Where?"

"Right here in my hotel. He slept two nights in the room right next door to this one."

"Is he still there?"

"No. He checked out."

Longarm could feel his heart starting to beat faster. "Did the man say where he was going?"

"No. He stayed to himself in his room most of the time."

"Describe him for me."

"He was of average height and awful rough looking. I didn't find him the least bit attractive like I do you and . . ."

"Hanna, tell me *exactly* what he looked like."

"Well, he wore a full beard. Brown it was, and shaggy. His hair was down to his shoulders and he was poorly dressed. Nothing remarkable about him at all except that silver inlaid rifle he carried and those fancy silver spurs that jingled when he walked."

"Did he register at your desk?"

"Well, of course."

Longarm started dressing.

"Where are you going, Custis? Are we done for to-night?"

"Hanna, it's almost morning and the rain has let up. I'm going looking for the man you described. Anything else you can tell me about him?"

"He limped and he had a nose caved in from a fight. I remember that he stank something awful. Our Chinaman said he refused his bath and stayed to his room drinking from a bottle of whiskey that was found empty in the morning. The Chinaman said the sheets on his bed were filthy and stained."

Longarm finished dressing and strapped on his gun. "Hanna, I can't thank you enough."

"You're coming back to me, ain't you? We had a real good time in bed."

"We did. But this man is bad, Hanna. As bad as they come, and I can't let him get away from me."

She crawled out of bed and stood before him, hands on wide hips, with each of her huge breasts hanging as big and loose as the udder of a milking cow. "I think he already did get away from you, Custis."

"What does that mean?"

"It means that I saw him heading for the train station before the storm arrived. He was catching the one that headed east."

"Toward Grants."

"And everywhere beyond," Hanna said. "Custis, your

man is gone and I'm here to stay, so why don't you just settle down and we'll take a nap, then we'll have breakfast and talk about what we want to do until we come back to this bed and have a good time."

Longarm realized that he was in the company of a very lonely and mentally unstable young woman in desperate need of support, despite her outwardly aggressive ways and physical size. "Hanna," he said in a gentle voice, "I've just *got* to leave you and find this man."

"If you do and you kill him, will you come back to me?"

"I'm afraid not," he said, deciding that the truth was kinder than a lie. "I like being a United States Marshal and living in Denver."

She was quiet for a long moment, then asked in a small voice, "You got a pretty wife waiting for you in Denver?"

"No. I've never married and probably never will."

"You should marry, Custis. So should I."

"I expect that is the truth, Hanna," he said as he grabbed up his bag and headed out the door. "But I'm just not the man you should think of marrying."

"If we're finished, then I'll find a good husband soon enough!"

He paused in the open doorway. "I know you will, Hanna. And I wish you the very best, and thank you for telling me about the man I'm hunting."

"Please don't let him kill you."

He heard a small sob coming from her and it was painful to realize that Hanna was so vulnerable and desperate for real love but would probably never find it.

"I won't let him kill me."

She straightened and lifted her chins. "And if you ever pass this way again and I'm not married . . . hell, even if I *am* married . . . come visit and make love to me."

"All right. I'd like that," Longarm said, and he knew that it was not entirely a bald-faced lie.

Longarm closed the door and practically ran down the dim staircase. He stopped in the lobby and searched the registration book looking for the name of a man he still did not know. And damned if he didn't find a name that rang a bell in his mind.

Henry Brody.

"The old Brody Gang," Longarm said to himself. "Could this possibly be one of them that survived Kenyon Chandler?"

It actually made a lot of sense. And that meant that the man might have connections back in the town of Grants. And maybe the killing of Kenyon and his wife hadn't really been random at all. Maybe this Henry Brody had been waiting for years to settle an old score with the famous old New Mexico lawman.

Outside, the rain had stopped and the dark, wet streets were filled with mud as Longarm slogged his way to the train station, only to find it closed up tight with nary a soul in sight. He was able to read a sign that said the trainmaster would return at eight o'clock in the morning.

Longarm pulled out his railroad pocket watch and checked the hour. It was half past five in the morning. Almost three hours until the train station opened and someone could tell him if the man that Hanna had described had bought a ticket and where he would get off the train.

"I'll go visit the two other stables," Longarm said to himself. "Henry Brody had to have left his horse somewhere. Probably sold it cheap. I can get even more information on the man and make good use of my time this morning."

Ignoring the sucking mud that pulled at his boots, Longarm plodded up the soggy street to rouse and speak to a couple of dishonest Gallup stablemen.

Chapter 13

A day after the rainstorm passed through northern New Mexico, Ned Corey and Lila Chandler reined in their horses and stared at towering, snowcapped Skull Mountain. After a while, Lila said, "Well, Ned, what do you think?"

"I had no idea the mountain was so *big*."

"I wish that map you got from Joshua Bixby was a whole lot more detailed," Lila told him. "Since it isn't, we could spend half our lives wandering around on Skull Mountain."

"I can see that now," Ned told her. He reached into his coat pocket and drew out the map. "Let's take a fresh look."

Lila studied the map and couldn't make a thing out of it. There wasn't even a compass penciled in to tell her north from south or east from west. All she could see were some crudely drawn peaks and side canyons and an X, which she knew marked the spot where Bixby had found his nuggets of almost pure gold.

"Does the map tell you anything new?" Ned Corey asked expectantly.

"No. In my opinion, it's pretty near worthless."

"Aw," Ned scoffed, "it's better than that!" His finger traced a line and then his eyes lifted to the top of Skull Mountain. "See there! That's got to be looking at Skull Mountain from about where we are now. So we're looking north and you can see that the gold find is on the south slope of this mountain."

"It isn't all that obvious to me," Lila said. "Where is the side canyon marked on that map?"

"Must be that one," Ned said, pointing. "I say that we start there and work our way up the south side of Skull Mountain. If we're lucky, we'll find the gold right away."

"I wouldn't be expecting that to happen so soon," Lila cautioned. "Even if the gold mine is on the south slope, that's still thousands of acres of heavy rock, timber, and debris that we'd have to navigate through."

"Do you really think it will be all that hard to cover?"

"I sure do. The altitude on that south slope is at least ten thousand feet, probably closer to eleven," Lila said. "That will make climbing tough for us and our horses. Up that high, the air will be thin and cold, the nights well below freezing. The place where Joshua Bixby found his gold could even be hidden under the snow near the top.

"I never told you or Marshal Long that this would be easy," Ned reminded her. "But we're talking about finding a *fortune*. I'd thought that having been raised in this county, you of all people wouldn't be intimidated by the forest or that big mountain."

"I'm not 'intimidated,'" Lila said, a little annoyed by his choice of words. "I'm respectful of Skull Mountain. Up on that wild south slope we can expect to find grizzlies and cougars, and they'll have a real interest in feasting on our horses."

"We can build a big bonfire and keep it going through the night."

"Do you know how much time and energy that will take? And we can't leave food around or they'll come for it, bonfire or no bonfire."

Ned swallowed nervously. "To be honest, I really didn't expect grizzly bears. I've never even seen one, and I thought they were mostly shot out of New Mexico years ago."

"Most have been," she said. "But big ones still haunt the highest mountains and most isolated high country. Ned, I'm not one to sound negative, but I'm trying to let you know that this is going to be a whole helluva lot harder than you're expecting. We could get killed up there in a rock slide or fall off a cliff."

"Good gawd, Lila! You're sounding about as dark as you could possibly be! This is probably our one chance in life to make a real fortune. If we find the gold, you can pay off your mortgage and keep the KC Ranch, maybe even build a new cabin and restock your herd."

"Believe me," she told him, "I'm well aware of that. But Ned, I'm curious as to what you'll do with your share of the money if Lady Luck favors us and we find our pot of gold."

Ned grinned. "First of all, I'd sell my newspaper and

move to a lower, warmer climate. Raton is hellish in the winter because it is so high. And then I'd probably buy a cattle ranch about like the KC."

She didn't bother to hide her surprise. "You'd want to be a cattle rancher?"

"I've always wanted to raise cattle."

"But you don't know a thing about ranching."

"Not so," Ned told her. "When I was a kid, I'd spend summers working for ranching people around Raton. I may not be a great horseback rider, but I'm adequate and I can throw a rope and brand a calf."

"For some reason, that amazes me."

"Well," Ned told her, "there's just a whole lot about me that would surprise and possibly amaze a girl like you."

"For instance?"

"For instance, I've been to New York City and I've been to San Francisco. My father used to take me places before he got old and settled. I like to travel and I've always wanted to visit Europe. If we find that gold that Bixby found up on that mountain, I'll go to Europe and travel in style."

"My oh my," Lila said, "you sure have some big ideas."

"The world is a big place and I mean to see it before I die."

"You can't go rambling around when you've got cows to look after," she warned.

"Sure you can, if you have enough money to hire good help," Ned argued. "I don't want a huge ranch. A smaller one like yours would be perfect, and the first thing I'd do is hire a foreman and build a house for him and his family. And I'd give him a share of the cattle ranch's annual profits just to keep him honest and happy enough to stay year after year."

"So you could go gallivantin' around the globe?"

"That's right," Ned said with a laugh to his voice. "Now, we'd better get busy climbing that mountain and make a camp before the sun goes down and it gets as cold as you've warned."

Later, beside an icy snow-fed creek, they found a fine campsite surrounded by pines and aspen that would give them protection on three sides from the wind. Close by there was a meadow, and their hobbled horses, weary from a long, hard climb up onto the south side of the mountain, now had rich grass to graze upon. There was even a small blue lake that held promise of trout.

"This will do very well," Lila said. "Gather firewood while I set up the camp and the cooking."

"All right."

Ned started to leave, but Lila stopped him. "Ned, cut a length of rope to make a sling so you can slip my rifle over your shoulder and carry an armload of firewood."

"You think I'll need to carry a rifle if I'm hardly out of sight?"

"There might be grizzly close by, and it wouldn't matter to the bear if you were in sight of this camp or not. If it was hungry or had a cub at its side, it might just take a notion to kill and eat you."

Ned's eyes widened and he nodded with understanding. "You make a good argument. But what about your protection? We've only got your rifle."

"I'm packing two pistols and I'm a pretty good tree climber in a pinch," she told him. "Just don't wander off very far."

"Believe you me, I sure won't."

Lila set to work with no idea if they would stay in this place one night or a week. It was late in the afternoon and the shadows were rapidly deepening. As she hurried to ready their campsite, she often paused to look and listen for danger. But the birds were still singing in the trees and an annoyed squirrel kept up its constant chatter, so she felt that there was no immediate danger.

Since the age of three, she had camped in high mountains with her legendary father and it had always been a happy experience. Kenyon Chandler had loved taking his daughter into the mountains where, he said, a man just naturally breathed a whole lot easier. He had been an expert hunter and enjoyed fishing these clear, cold lakes and streams. Lila had brought fishing line and hooks from her ranch, and now that her camp was in order, she dug for grubs or worms, eager to see if she could catch them a string of fresh fish.

"How much firewood do we need tonight?" Ned asked, carrying in a second armload and dumping it at their camp.

"Depends on if there are grizzly bears in the neighborhood and how badly you want a good night's sleep."

"I'll get more wood," he told her.

"I'm going down to see if that little lake has any hungry fish."

Lila found a rock beside the lake, then used a pocketknife to fashion a pole from a branch. She tied her fishing line and hook-and-baited it with a worm from the soft, mushy ground, noting that fish were jumping at sundown.

Almost at once she began to pull in fine speckled trout. Big, fat, hungry fish that would go down mighty easy after being panfried over her campfire. Lila had brought corn meal, flour, salt and pepper, and potatoes, and danged if this wasn't going to be a fine meal. She cleaned the fish by the lakeside and carried them to her camp on a string.

Later that evening, sitting around their crackling campfire and after eating all the fish that they wanted, Lila and Ned spread out their bedrolls and prepared to retire. The stars were so bright that it seemed as if they could pluck them from the night sky, and the air had gotten cold but there was no wind rustling through the pines.

"This is really nice," Ned told her from across the fire.

"It is that," Lila agreed.

"Did your father and mother ever bring you up here on Skull Mountain to camp when you were a little girl?"

"No. We just always seemed to find other mountains. And there was something about the name Skull Mountain that made me prefer to stay away from it."

"Yeah," Ned agreed. "Skull Mountain isn't a name that brings comforting thoughts to a person."

"My father came up here alone, though. Once, he chased a pair of Mexican bandits up here, but he lost them in the rocks up near the summit. Couple of months later, those two Mexicans stupidly rode into Grants, and my father arrested both of them without a shot being fired."

"What were they accused of?"

"Rustling three milk cows. Father took them to Albuquerque to stand trial, and I think they were sent to jail for six months."

"I wish I'd known your parents," Ned told her as he fed the fire. "I'm sure I would have liked them."

"You'd have loved my mother," Lila said, "but father was a hard and critical man. He was always a little curt with strangers and not easy to talk to. Ned, I'm not sure that you and he would have gotten along at first."

"I can get along with most everyone," Ned told her. "Except my own father."

"Fathers can be tough," Lila told him with a yawn. "We're going to have a long, hard day tomorrow, so good night."

Somewhere in the middle of the night they heard a mountain lion scream again and again. Lila awoke thinking maybe it was a warning that there was danger all around this place. But it was a warning that she and Ned would ignore for the chance to find Bixby's gold. Enough gold to pay off her mortgage and restock their ranch with good cows and a fine, pureblooded bull. Lila stared up at the heavens and reminded herself once more not to let her hopes get the better of her. The chances of finding the gold on this huge and foreboding mountain were not as good as Ned thought, and she had had enough heartache and disappointments lately to last the rest of her lifetime.

"Ned, wake up and have some coffee!" she said to the man who still slept soundly even though the sun was struggling off the eastern horizon.

Ned groaned and climbed out of his blankets. "It sure got cold last night. I felt like I was freezing."

"It *was* cold! Have some coffee and let's saddle the horses and start searching for that gold mine."

"How about some breakfast first?" he asked, rubbing the sleep from his eyes.

"There's some jerky you can chew on along with my hot coffee," Lila told him. "But as for me, I'm saddling up and riding."

"You sure are in a big hurry."

"I am," she confessed. "This camp and that lake are beautiful. Couldn't be nicer. But . . ." Lila's words trailed off into silence.

"But what?" Ned asked, pulling on his boots and coming over to pour himself some coffee.

"But there is something about this place that gives me the spooks," Lila blurted. "There's just a feeling in my bones now that everything up here is not right or as it should be."

Ned looked all around and pointed down at the placid lake. "That's a queer way to feel about such a beautiful setting."

"I know, but the sooner we find the gold and leave, the better I'll feel. I only wish Custis was with us right now."

Ned sipped his coffee with a frown. "Your lawman friend ought to be up here in a couple of days, and I think that we can take care of ourselves until then. Heck! We might even have found the gold by the time Custis arrives."

"If we do, he'll still get a third."

"That doesn't seem entirely right," Ned hedged. "I mean, *I'm* the one with the map, and if he isn't even here to help us find—"

"Ned," Lila said, cutting off his words, "Custis is hunting for the man who murdered my parents. He isn't off having a good time."

"You're right." Ned stood up and drained his coffee. "Don't worry. Custis Long will get his third of the gold. I made that agreement and I'll stand by it."

"You wouldn't have any choice but to stand by it," Lila said, making her meaning crystal clear.

"Lila, can I ask you something real personal?"

"You can ask but I might not answer."

"Are you in *love* with Custis Long?"

She considered the question carefully before she answered. "I think I am," she replied. "I asked him to marry me and give up his badge."

"He doesn't seem like the kind of a man that would ever make a cattle rancher."

"Neither do you, but yesterday you said differently."

Ned had to smile. "I guess I did at that. But I'd hate to

see your feelings get hurt if Custis wraps up things here in New Mexico and goes back to Denver, leaving you with ashes for dreams."

"Don't you go worrying about my feelings, Ned Corey. I've just discovered both of my parents have been murdered and I'm only a couple short weeks away from losing the KC Ranch . . . the home that I've spent most of my life helping my mother and father build from nothing. So the way that I see my life right now is that I've very little else to lose."

"I understand. I'm sorry if I spoke out of turn."

Lila's face softened. "It's all right, Ned. After all, if we hadn't met you and you hadn't trusted Custis and myself, then we wouldn't be here with the possibility of striking it rich. So rest assured that I view your friend-ship and our association as one of the few positive things in my life right now."

"That's a very nice way to put it, Lila."

"Good," she said. "Then finish up that coffee, grab a hunk of beef jerky, and let's start hunting for gold!"

Chapter 14

Longarm's boots were clotted with mud and he was in a foul mood when he arrived at a run-down livery stable. Off to the east the sun was just a pale line across the eastern horizon and the air was cold and crisp.

"Hello?" he called at the door of the stable barn. "Anybody here?"

There was no answer, so Longarm threw open the big double doors and stepped into the dark barn. There were only two horses inside, and after he lit matches, he could see that neither was the one that he'd trailed most of the way from the KC Ranch. After closing the barn doors, he headed up the muddy street until he came to the only stable left that he had not yet visited.

"Hello?" he shouted from beside the barn door. "Anyone awake in there?"

"Go away!"

Longarm had no intention of going anywhere. He was quite certain now that the man Hanna had described in his hotel room was the killer he was hunting, but finding the man's horse would be an additional confirmation of that fact.

"I'm a United States Marshal and I'm coming in, so don't shoot!"

Longarm heard curses as he opened the door and stepped into a filthy barn reeking of urine and horse shit. "Need a lantern!"

"Go straight to hell and find it!"

Longarm was in no mood for being trifled with. He saw a lantern hanging on a nail got it lit. The barn wasn't big and he saw no horses inside. Maybe, he thought, there was a corral out behind the barn.

"Who the hell are you?" a tall, heavy-set man demanded as he raked a dirty paw across his even dirtier face and held a shotgun pointed at Longarm.

"I told you that I'm a United States Marshal."

"I don't like the law and I don't like being waked up at the crack of dawn, so get the hell off my property."

Longarm raised his hand and removed his hat. "Didn't mean to alarm you," he said with an apologetic smile.

The man cocked back the hammer of his shotgun. "Git!"

Longarm pretended to drop his hat to the dirt floor, and when he bent as if to pick it up, he grabbed a handful of horse turds and hurled them into the liveryman's face.

"What the . . . ?"

Longarm batted the shotgun aside and it blew a hole

in the barn's roof. He delivered a short, wicked right cross into the man's jaw that lifted him to his toes. The liveryman staggered and Longarm slammed a thundering left hook to his gut. The man's mouth flew open as his eyes bugged in his agony. Finishing him off, Longarm dropped the man to the ground with a straight right to the nose that broke it with a cracking sound.

"Get up!" Longarm ordered, grabbing the smoking shotgun and hurling it into a pile of straw.

"You broke my damned nose!" the man wailed, cupping it in his hands as blood ran between his fingers. "Gawdamn you!"

"Next time you hold a gun on a federal officer you'll probably get shot dead, you stupid sonofabitch! Now stand up and quit your sniveling."

The liveryman swayed to his feet and Longarm pushed him roughly up against the side of the barn. In very few words he described the horse he was tracking. "Is that animal here? Did Henry Brody sell it to you?"

"He didn't say his damned name and I didn't ask! The horse you're lookin' for is out back in a corral with some others that I own. A dun gelding. I bought him two days ago."

"If you'd have told me that right away, you wouldn't have gotten your beak busted," Longarm snorted. "Tell me everything the man who sold you the horse said."

"Let me get a wet bandage for my nose!"

"All right."

Minutes later, the liveryman was holding a wet rag that he'd just soaked in cold water to his nose. His eyes

were streaming tears, and as he described the man who'd
sold him the dun horse, he sagged against the edge of a
horse watering trough.

"Did he tell you his name?"

"No. He just wanted money for the horse and saddle.
Said he needed the money for a train ticket."

"Where to?"

"Hell if I know or care!"

"All right," Longarm said, turning on his heel to
leave.

"What about my broken nose?"

Longarm turned back to the man. "What about it?"

"It'll cost me to see a doctor and have it bandaged
and set straight."

"If I were you," Longarm said, "I'd just leave that
nose the way it is now. As ugly as you are, it might even
be an improvement."

"Damn you, Marshal!" The man cursed as Longarm
headed for the Cattleman's Café figuring he had time for
breakfast before going to the train station and seeing if
he could learn exactly how far Henry Brody's ticket was
carrying him eastward.

The train station manager asked Longarm to show him a
badge, and once he did, the man was ready to help. "The
fella you are lookin' for bought a one-way ticket to
Grants, New Mexico."

"When is the next train leaving for Grants?" Longarm
asked.

"I'm afraid that won't be until this evening. They had

a bridge wash out just the other side of Winslow, Arizona, and the eastbound is running behind schedule."

"How many miles is it to Grants?"

"About seventy following the tracks."

"Damn!" Longarm muttered, thinking that it would take him too long to ride Lila's palomino all the way to Grants and he'd half kill himself and the animal doing it.

"What's your problem, Marshal?"

"I rode a friend's horse here from Grants and she thinks too much of it for me to leave or sell it to someone here in Gallup."

"For five dollars you can load the animal on the eastbound, and if you stay with it in a cattle boxcar, we won't charge you any extra to ride to Grants."

"Then that's what I'll do," Longarm decided. "Any chance that the eastbound will make up some time and come early?"

"No chance at all," the train station manager told him. "But even if it runs a little later than expected, you'll still be in Grants long before daylight tomorrow morning."

"All right," Longarm told the man. "I'll take your offer. Where should I have my horse standing and ready to be loaded into a cattle car when the train pulls into your station?"

The man pointed to the west. "Right up yonder, and I'll tell the conductor to hold the train. Your horse will load all right, won't he? Don't want to hold up the eastbound any longer for any fool or cantankerous horse."

"He'll load," Longarm promised, not at all sure if

loading the palomino into a cattle car would be a problem or not.

"Fair enough, then. I'll take your five dollars, Marshal. And I hope you get your man in Grants."

"I expect that I will. Would you mind describing him for me?"

The train station manager described Henry Brody exactly as Hanna and the angry liveryman had described him. Brown shoulder-length hair, dirty, and with a fist-busted nose. He ended by saying, "I wished I could have put your man in a cattle car to Grants."

"Why is that?"

"He stunk to high heavens!"

Longarm almost smiled before he bought his ticket and headed back to the Frontier Hotel to get his belongings from his room and maybe have a final romp or two with the buxom and frisky Miss Hanna Fetter.

Chapter 15

Halfway up Skull Mountain, the wind started blowing hard from the north, which meant it was straight into their faces. Lila and Ned felt the icy blast and lowered their heads, always trying to keep their horses in the protection of the pines. The trees were whipping back and forth and the sky was dark and foreboding.

"Damn this foul weather!" Ned called from behind as Lila guided her blue roan through the forest, climbing steadily higher. She had no idea where to start looking for Joshua Bixby's gold strike, but she figured she would see signs of it if the snow didn't start falling. The pine forest was so thick that there was no way of knowing how far they were from the snow, but Lila figured it was still another thousand feet or more to the summit.

The only encouraging thing was that they seemed to have come upon a trail, though Lila had no idea if it was made by wild game or Joshua Bixby. Having no other ideas, she had let Blueberry follow that trail steadily upward, and her pack animals followed along behind.

The wind finally abated late in the afternoon and the squall seemed to have passed. The sun came out and the sky turned a clear, cobalt blue. Several times deer bounded through the trees, and once she saw a huge bull elk sail over a fallen tree. So far there was no sign of any grizzly bears, and for that Lila was grateful.

Late that afternoon they came to a low line of sandstone cliffs and Lila could see that they curved to the east and into a canyon about a mile away. At the same time the trail that she was following veered in that direction and she saw a discarded and rusty tobacco tin.

"Look, Ned! See that tobacco tin? Someone has been up here not so long ago."

"How do you know it hasn't been there for years?"

"Up in this high, snowy country, a tin like that wouldn't last more than a few years."

"Think it belonged to Joshua Bixby?"

"You tell me. Did he smoke?"

"Yeah," Ned replied, climbing down from the chestnut to examine the tin. "And this was his brand of tobacco!"

"Then maybe we really are on the trail to his gold mine. If so, I'm afraid that we're not the first."

Ned looked up at her with a frown. "What is that supposed to mean?"

"It means that I've seen some fresh horse tracks on this trail. Because of the hard rainstorm we had a few days ago, and others before that, most all of those tracks have been washed out or covered over by deer tracks.

But unless I'm badly mistaken, a couple of riders have been up this trail during the past few weeks."

"Damn!" Ned cried, eyes reaching up the trail. "How could . . . ?"

"I have no earthly idea," Lila said, cutting him off. "But my guess is that if we keep riding, we'll get some answers. I don't suppose that old Bixby filed a mining claim on this mountain."

"No."

"That's what I thought," Lila said. "Mount up and let's push on until near dark. But keep your eyes peeled and listen sharply."

"Don't worry about that," Ned assured. "I just hope that someone doesn't find that gold strike before we can!"

"Me, too," Lila said.

Now there was a sense of urgency that had not been there earlier as they pushed their animals hard up the southern face of Skull Mountain and into a deep canyon that seemed as though it might run right up close to the summit. Lila kept bending over in her saddle looking for more evidence of horsemen, but she didn't see any more tracks or discarded tobacco cans. Even so, she felt as if she and Ned were riding into trouble, and she wished more than ever that Longarm was at their sides.

Afternoon came and found them still pushing hard as the light died early and the canyon's walls leaned in ever closer. "Let's make a cold camp," Lila suggested, reining her horse across a cold, swift creek into the forest as she searched for a good camp.

Ned nodded in weary agreement. His young face looked haggard, and Lila supposed it was partly because of their long and difficult riding, but also because now he was anxious about the chance that other men had already found old Joshua Bixby's gold mine.

That night they camped without a fire, and because they were at a higher elevation, the night was freezing. And without hot food or a campfire, they were miserable until morning's first light.

"The snow can't be much higher," Ned commented as they tended to their horses.

"I know. We're almost to the tree line and well over ten thousand feet. It makes you wonder how someone could have come up here and found gold this high."

"Yeah, it does," Ned agreed.

"Let's grain the horses," she said. "We'll lead them the rest of the way up this canyon on foot."

"Why?"

"Because," Lila explained, "if there are men up in this canyon working a gold mine and we just ride in on them, then we make easy targets. But if we're on foot, we have a better chance to survive. And besides, we'll be at the snow level soon, and after that there isn't much point of going higher."

"We can't quit."

"I'm not saying we'll quit," Lila replied patiently. "I'm just saying that I have a bad feeling about what is up ahead and I don't want to be sitting my horse like a storefront window mannequin as an easy target."

"All right then, let's hike," Ned snapped with irritation. "But the air is so thin up here that it will be hard."

"Life is hard, so quit complaining."

Ned shot her a go-to-hell look.

Lila was in the front leading Blueberry when suddenly the animal snorted in fear and spun around, trying to retreat. Lila grabbed her saddle horn as the frightened animal plunged and smashed into her pack animal, which then slammed into Ned and his chestnut gelding.

"What the . . . ?"

Lila knew what it was even before she saw the big sow and her cinnamon-colored bear cub. "Grizzly!" she hissed. "Hang on to your horses, Ned, and back on down the trail!"

The sow was rummaging around in an abandoned campsite. Now she caught the scent of humans and horses and gave a snort, then reared back on her hind legs, warily sniffing the wind. Lila knew that these bears were far keener with their noses than their eyes, and she hoped she was still far enough away that the sow did not see her and feel that her cub was being threatened.

Lila got Blueberry and her packhorse under control and she turned and hurried back down the trail following the retreating Ned Corey. When they rounded a bend and disappeared from the grizzly's sight, she stopped and caught her breath, heart hammering.

"Will it come down that trail after us?" Ned asked, his face pinched with anxiety.

"I don't think so. The sow caught our scent, and since we were still quite a ways off, my guess is that she'll lead her cub away to safety rather than come after us."

"But you don't know that for certain."

"No, I don't," Lila confessed. "A mother bear with a cub can be unpredictable." She pulled her rifle from her saddle scabbard, adding, "If the sow is coming after us, our horses will be the first to know. Just hang on to them as long as you can and let's wait this out."

Ned unholstered his six-gun. "I sure hope there isn't going to be a fight," he said.

"I think we're going to be all right," Lila assured him. "Let's just wait it out for an hour and then I'll hike up the trail with my rifle and see if the sow and her cub are still at that abandoned campsite."

"You saw a campsite!"

"I did," Lila replied.

"Well, did you also see a gold mine?"

"No. But I only had a moment to glimpse up there."

"Then how do you know it was a campsite?"

"Ned," Lila said, "just shut up and let's listen in case that grizzly is heading down the trail in our direction."

Ned nodded and clenched his jaw. The horses were nervous, but no longer terrified. An hour passed and Lila finally handed her reins to Ned, saying, "Just hold the horses and wait for me to come back."

"But what if the grizzly is circling around to attack us from behind!"

"She won't be doing that, Ned."

"Are you sure?"

"I am. Now be still and calm. I'll just hike up to that bend in the trail and have another look."

"Be careful!"

"Believe me, I sure will."

Lila walked cautiously up the thin mountain trail, and when she came to the bend, she crouched and peered back up the canyon. The big sow and her cub were gone. She waited ten minutes, and when she was sure that the danger was past, she hiked back to Ned.

"The grizzly and her cub are gone. Let's go!"

They mounted their horses, grabbed their lead ropes to the packhorses, and rode fast up the trail. "I see a mine and an empty camp!" Lila called back.

Both of them still had their weapons in their fists and Ned called up to her, "Are you sure it's *empty*?"

"Yes."

Lila spurred her horse into a trot and suddenly saw something a lot more chilling than she could have ever imagined finding on Skull Mountain.

"Holy cow!" Ned whispered, hauling up on his reins and staring slack-jawed. "Are those *human* skeletons?"

"I'm afraid so."

Lila dismounted and, with her Winchester still clenched tightly in her fist, she went to stand over four broken and chewed-up skeletons. She wouldn't have known for certain that there were four if it hadn't been for the skulls, because the body bones had been scattered all over what had once been a prospector's camp.

"What do you think happened!" Ned cried. "Did that grizzly kill and then eat them all?"

"Not unless she was carrying a rifle," Lila replied, her

voice quiet and low. "Because what I'm seeing are bullet holes in the skulls."

Ned swallowed hard and looked wildly around them, waving his pistol in his hand.

"Take it easy, Ned. These four were shot several weeks ago," Lila pronounced.

"How can you tell it's been that long?"

"Over the years I've seen the skulls of a lot of dead horses and cattle," she replied. "And I know for certain that these skulls still haven't been picked clean by the ants, beetles, and other insects."

"Oh damn," Ned whispered. "Do you think it's possible that old Joshua Bixby somehow got the drop on these four and shot them to death for trying to steal his claim?"

"I don't know," Lila said, shaking her head. "I never met Bixby, but you did. Do you think he was capable of killing all of these men?"

"No." Ned dismounted and threw his hands up in the air with exasperation. "To be honest, Lila, I really haven't any idea."

"Then maybe someone else killed these four. Or perhaps Bixby had a partner or two when they came upon his mine."

"Or maybe they were his partners and Bixby surprised and then murdered them so he could have all the gold for himself," Ned mused aloud.

"It's a mystery we might never unravel," Lila told the newspaperman. "But I do know one thing for certain."

"What's that?"

Lila used the toe of her boot to turn the skulls so that the bullet holes were all clearly in view. "Someone coldly executed these four. Most likely there was more than one man who did it. Several, I'd guess."

Ned looked away and said, "At least we found Joshua Bixby's gold mine."

"I hope not."

"Why do you say that?" Ned asked.

"Because if it is where those gold nuggets came from, then the mine has been picked clean or the murderers would still be here working with picks and shovels."

Ned slowly nodded his head with understanding. "Yeah, I see what you mean."

"So either the gold has been mined out of that tunnel . . . or it was never there in the first place."

Ned seemed to shiver as he studied all the scattered human bones. "Let's find out right now," he said, starting for the mine tunnel. "Because if the gold isn't in that mine, then I want to get out of this damned haunted canyon just as fast as our horses will carry us."

"Makes a hell of a lot of good sense to me," Lila told him as she tore her eyes away from the four skulls and hurried toward the dark mine tunnel. "But before we go into that mine, we're going to need a torch for light."

"I've got matches."

"That's not good enough," she said. "Find a dry branch and then rub it against a pine for the pitch. We're probably going to need to be in there for more than a few minutes."

"All right."

While Ned went to make them a torch, Lila tied the horses up to trees. They could still smell the grizzly and her cub, and the animals were skittish and afraid. Lila soothed them as she waited.

"What's the matter with those horses?" Ned asked.

"They want to get out of here even worse than we do," Lila replied as she took the torch and headed for the mine with a feeling of dread sitting down deep in the pit of her stomach.

Chapter 16

It was three o'clock in the morning when Longarm unloaded Lila's palomino gelding from the rattling and drafty cattle car. Longarm was exhausted from standing with the nervous animal all the way between Gallup and Grants. The seventy or so miles he'd just covered in a cold cattle car had seemed to him more like five hundred, but now as he led the horse down the ramp and waved at the conductor, he was glad that he had decided not to ride that distance. If he had done so, he'd still be facing a long horseback ride tomorrow.

Longarm tightened his cinch and rode up the dark street into town. He would get a hotel room and sleep for a few hours, then start looking for Henry Brody. Longarm was almost certain that the killer would be easy to find, considering the full description he'd been given of the man by people in Gallup. There was no telling why Brody had suddenly decided to return to Grants. Perhaps he had found a seller for the inlaid Winchester and spurs in Gallup and was now returning to lie low or celebrate. Or perhaps he was coming back to meet with someone who had hired him to carry out the KC Ranch killings. Until Longarm found Henry Brody and managed to capture him alive, there was just no way of getting answers to those puzzling questions.

The sun was high when Longarm awoke late that morning in the Pinto Pony Hotel. He yawned, stretched, and dressed. There was a mirror in his room, and when he glanced at it, he was shocked and sorry.

I sure look like I've been dragged through hell, he thought, rubbing the whiskers on his face and noting the dark bags under his eyes.

Longarm dressed and went downstairs for coffee. As expected, the hotel's genial owner, Homer Monroe, was holding court in his restaurant.

"Well, well," Homer bellowed. "Look what the cat dragged in this morning! Marshal Long, excuse me for saying so, but you need a bath, a shave, and a set of clean clothes. What the hell have you been up to these last few days?"

"Homer," Longarm said, taking a seat at the man's table, "you don't want to know."

"Sure I do!"

"I'm afraid that I can't tell you just yet."

The man's round face lost its habitual smile. "That sounds like bad news coming."

"I'm afraid that it is." Longarm forced a weary smile. "I'm looking for a man."

"A very evil one, I assume."

"That's right." Longarm described Henry Brody in detail. He ended by saying, "I can't tell you why, but I need to arrest and then talk to him."

"What has he done? Can't you at least tell me that?"

Longarm was very reluctant to tell this man that his old friend, Kenyon Chandler, and his wife had been murdered at their small cattle ranch. "Homer, how about you buy me a big breakfast and coffee, then we'll talk where no one can overhear us?"

"That will do," Homer said. "Let's go sit at that far table by the window. Steak and eggs all right?"

"Sure," Longarm said, "and biscuits and gravy. But mainly coffee, lots of strong coffee."

"Yeah," Homer said, "you look like you had a short night's sleep."

"You don't know the half of it," Longarm said cryptically.

A half hour later and on his third cup of Homer's good coffee, Longarm was feeling almost half human. "I'm looking for this man named Henry Brody that I described because I have some very sad news to tell you."

Homer Monroe blinked and sat up in his chair. "Shoot."

"Brody murdered Kenyon and his wife out at their KC Ranch."

"No!"

"I'm afraid so," Longarm told the shocked hotel owner. "From what I could see, the couple must have been surprised. I think that Brody caught Mrs. Chandler first and then I suspect he forced Kenyon to throw down a weapon or his wife would be shot."

"But the bastard shot them both anyway!" Monroe said bitterly. "Is that what you think happened out there?"

"Yes."

"And he killed them for *what*?"

"Maybe just for what the man could steal. Maybe for more than that." Longarm shrugged. "I won't know until I arrest and question Brody."

"What can I do to help?"

"Have you seen a man that fits that description?"

"I wish I could tell you that I had."

"Don't worry about it, Homer. I'll find him, and it shouldn't take all that long."

"I'd be glad to help."

Longarm shook his head. "I'd feel better if you just stayed out of it."

"But Kenyon and his wife were my dear friends!"

"I know. But if you want me to find out everything, I have to do this alone and my way."

"Does Lila know her parents were murdered?"

"Sure."

Homer Monroe shook his head and then banged his meaty fist on the table so hard that coffee jumped from their cups. "Damn!" he whispered, using his napkin to wipe away fresh tears. "They didn't deserve to die like that."

"No," Longarm agreed. "They did not. But it's done and I know who the killer is. The only question is why he committed the murders."

"For Kenyon's fancy rifle and spurs! And he probably found some cash and other things in the house."

"Yeah," Longarm said. "But something is telling me that he might have murdered that old couple for other reasons."

"Like what?"

"I don't know yet," Longarm told the distraught hotelman. "But I sure as shootin' aim to find out this morning. This town doesn't have a jail, does it?"

"No. We never got around to building one. But we've got one hell of a good hanging tree."

"I'll keep that in mind. Can I use my hotel room to question Brody after I've arrested him?"

"Sure, if I can be there as a witness."

"Agreed," Longarm told the man. He used his napkin, finished off his coffee, and pushed up from his chair. "Thanks for the breakfast, Homer. I really needed it this morning."

"Where are you going to start looking for this murdering sonofabitch?"

"The saloons," Longarm told the man as he left him sitting in misery.

Chapter 17

It didn't take much time to find out that the killer, Henry Brody, had left Grants at dawn that same morning with the town's wealthy banker and landowner, John Jacob, along with two other heavily armed horsemen.

A well-known town drunk and panhandler named Moses Whitman had seen the four men quietly riding up a back alley and it had seemed odd even to Whitman's whiskey-befuddled brain that the four were sneaking out of Grants. And what Moses Whitman found even more puzzling was that they were leading a packhorse as if they were going to be away awhile.

"What else can you tell me?" Longarm asked the old man, whose liver-spotted hands were trembling for the desperate need of a drink.

"You got some money for old Moses? Need a drink or two mighty bad."

Longarm gave Whitman two dollars. "Moses, can you tell me anything more?"

Whitman's fingers clenched the silver dollars like the talons of an eagle. "Nope. Just that they all looked like they were up to serious business. Can I go now, Marshal?"

"Where did they leave from?"

"The Monarch Livery Stable. Mr. Jacob, he doesn't own a horse of his own. Never even seen him ride one until this morning. He ain't a good rider. But the other men all were."

"And you're *sure* that one of them was Henry Brody?"

"Yes, sir! I knew the Brody Gang when I was a younger man, and Henry was the last of a bad lot. He was only a boy when his pa and uncles were gunned down by Marshal Chandler many years ago, but he was already rotten to the core. Meanest kid I ever saw or ever want to see."

"Moses, thanks for telling me this. You might have saved some lives. Now why don't you go to the Pinto Pony Hotel and tell Mr. Monroe that I sent you to him. Tell Mr. Monroe to give you a room and a hot bath, and then a good breakfast of steak, eggs, and coffee."

Moses managed a weak smile. "Marshal, I can't afford all that!"

"Tell Mr. Monroe that I'll pay for it when I come back to Grants in a few days."

"But I need a drink a whole lot more'n I do food or a bath!"

Longarm put his arm across the drunkard's thin shoulders. "How old are you, Moses?"

The drunkard had to think hard for a moment before he mumbled, "Forty . . . forty-somethin'."

The man looked to be in his sixties and not far removed from a pauper's grave. "Listen to me, Moses. You've got to stop drinking so hard. You need to eat more and take better care of yourself or you're not going to last much longer."

"Yes, sir."

Longarm was almost certain that Moses Whitman would take his two dollars and go straight to a saloon rather than the Pinto Pony, so he led the old man to the hotel. When Homer Monroe appeared, Longarm said, "Moses has just saved me a lot of time this morning. He says he saw your banker, John Jacob, Henry Brody, and two other well-armed men leading a packhorse out of town at daybreak."

The hotel owner blinked. "But what . . . ?"

"They were headed *north*," Longarm emphasized, cutting off the man's question. "That means they are either going to the KC Ranch to finish off their bloody business . . . or they're going up to Skull Mountain to kill Lila and Ned. Either way, I've got to overtake them."

The hotel owner glanced at a big wall clock in his hotel lobby. "If they rode out of Grants at daybreak, that means that they have at least a five-hour start on you."

"I know," Longarm said grimly. "I'm going to have to ride like the devil was on my tail and hope that they don't kill Miss Chandler and that newspaperman from Raton before I can overtake them."

"I'll come with you!"

"Sorry, Homer, but I'll be riding too hard."

"I can keep up!"

"I don't think so," Longarm said, turning to leave.

"Dammit, Marshal, I've got a racehorse in the barn and I can ride him like a Comanche!"

Longarm sincerely doubted that was true. But he said, "I'll be riding Lila's tall palomino to her ranch. If she and Ned Corey aren't there, then I'll ride on to Skull Mountain."

"You got a rifle?"

"I do."

"Well, so do I," Homer Monroe said, "and it might surprise you to know that I've used it to win at least a dozen turkeys in local shooting contests over the past five years. So I can ride and I can shoot, despite how I may appear to you physically. And Kenyon was my best friend. I want to go along and help. You'll need my help coming up against four men, dammit!"

"All right," Longarm conceded, also glancing at the hotel's big wall clock. "I'll give you a half hour. Not a minute more, mind you. Then I'm leaving."

"I'll meet you at the stable where you put your horse up," Monroe said. "And I got a few friends here in town that we can call upon to help us."

"Sorry, but there is just no time to round them up," Longarm snapped as he whirled around and headed for the nearest general store to hastily buy some supplies and desperately needed ammunition.

Chapter 18

"There's no gold in here and probably never was," Lila said as they stood at the end of the long mine tunnel with the pine torch flickering in Ned's upheld hand.

"But if this isn't the place where Joshua Bixby found gold, then where . . . ?"

"I don't know," Lila replied, anxious to get back into the sunlight. "But if those men outside were murdered for Joshua Bixby's gold, then the strike must be close by."

"That's probably it," Ned agreed. "Bixby must have dug this tunnel over the years and maybe even did it with the help of those four whose bones we found outside. This tunnel is too big and long to have been dug out by Bixby alone."

"Makes sense," Lila said, emerging from the suffocating confinement of the mining tunnel. "And my guess is that Joshua Bixby was probably off someplace nearby when this camp was attacked and the four men were captured. Maybe whoever did it tried to make the four talk, and when they refused, they were executed one by one."

"We'll never know," Ned told her as they stood looking down again at the bullet-riddled skulls. "But I tell you this . . . Skull Mountain has re-earned its name. All I want to do is get far away from here."

"I can't do that," Lila told him, "because I firmly believe that old Joshua Bixby was telling you the truth on his deathbed. And I also think that the map he managed to scribble with his dying hand was probably the best that he could do in return for your kindness during his final hours."

"So you think that the gold mine still exists?"

"I do," Lila replied. "And so does whoever murdered these four men. Ned, get that map out and let's ride up to the head of this canyon and just sit. I think we really need to reexamine Bixby's map and put our heads together and think this out. My feeling is that the real gold mine can't be far away. Not far at all. If it was, then these four wouldn't have been executed."

Ned's chin dipped in agreement. "This death camp is making my skin crawl. Let's get it out of our sight."

"Agreed," Lila said, mounting her horse and hurrying up toward the head of the narrowing canyon.

Ten minutes later they found a rocky clearing ringed by snow and huge boulders. Lila dismounted and tied her horse to a scrubby and wind-bent pine along with their other horses.

"Do you feel better up here?" she asked, when Ned

was seated beside her on a boulder with the map spread out across on his lap.

"Much better," the newspaperman answered as he gazed back down the canyon.

"So let's go over everything that Joshua Bixby told you on his deathbed, and then let's study that map again."

"Do you really think that will help?"

"How can it hurt?" Lila asked. "We've come this far and found four dead men. There has got to be some reasonable answer for all of this killing."

For the next hour, Ned recounted everything that the dying prospector had told him and then they carefully, even painstakingly, went over every single detail on Bixby's poorly drawn map.

"What is this horseshoe-shaped line with the bar across the top of its toe?" Lila asked, tracing the lines with her forefinger.

"I don't know," Ned admitted. "I never could figure out what Joshua meant by putting it there."

Lila frowned, thinking hard. "What if it was Bixby's attempt to define this very canyon and . . ."

"And the bar at the top is the *snow line* just above us!"

"Yes!"

Lila could feel her heart suddenly thumping in her chest. "If that's the case, the snow up on the summit would have receded at least a couple of hundred feet since the map was drawn, meaning that . . ."

Ned was so excited that he cut her off in mid-sentence, blurting, "That we are sitting almost where Joshua made an X to mark the spot of his gold discovery."

"That's right, Ned." Lila looked around at all the boulders at the top of the canyon. "I think that what we're looking for is to be found among these big rocks. Perhaps even underneath or between them."

"A mine?"

Lila shook her head. "Not if it's close. More likely we're searching for gold that was washed down from the summit of Skull Mountain over many long centuries. My guess is we're looking for a rock close by with a vein of gold. That's what I think Joshua Bixby found up here on Skull Mountain."

"I hope it's a lot more than just a vein."

"Me, too."

Lila stood and studied the boulder field. "I think your old friend found those gold nuggets somewhere close to where we are standing. Let's see if we can find it or at least some evidence that Bixby has been here."

"What kind of evidence?"

"A tobacco tin belonging to Joshua Bixby would be evidence enough to tell us we are close to his gold discovery."

"All right," Ned told her. "Let's start looking!"

"If we don't find it before dark, we'll make a camp up here and give it another day or two," Lila decided. "I'm almost certain the gold is here among this field of huge boulders."

All that day they searched, and just before dark, deep under an immense boulder, they found the source of Joshua Bixby's vein of pure gold. They'd have missed it entirely had it not been for another tobacco tin lying wedged among some rocks above.

"Look at the bottom of that rock!" Lila cried after squeezing down under an immense boulder and staring at its underside. "Lots of quartz and a thin ribbon of gold!"

Ned climbed down to join her and both of them stared at the fine thread of gold that ran under the rock until it disappeared where it could not be seen or reached.

"But the vein is so *thin*," Ned lamented. "I was hoping for something really big—deep and wide."

"It's big enough to scratch out a small fortune for us," Lila told him. "See where Bixby used his rock pick to break off nuggets? Maybe they were the biggest of the nuggets, but only time will tell."

"But it's so close and dangerous under this boulder."

"It's probably been here a long, long time," Lila said reassuringly. "And I'm no prospector, but I've talked to a lot of them over the years, and they've often described finding gold embedded in granite and quartz boulders. Sometimes a few nuggets of pure gold like corn kernels will be protruding from the rock, and I'll bet those are the easy ones that Joshua extracted and then later gave you in repayment for your kindness to him as he was dying."

"But what about those four dead men we found?"

"I have no idea who they are," she told him. "Maybe how they died will forever be a mystery. All we can do now is get our rock picks and go to work extracting as much gold as we can before our supplies run out and we have to ride back to Grants for more."

Ned studied the huge boulder hanging overhead. "Do you think there's any chance that this thing could break loose and drop on us?"

"There's always a slight risk," Lila told him. "Let's stop fretting and not waste any more daylight."

"All right," Ned told her. "But that rock must weigh as much as a cathedral, and if it . . ."

"Stop it!" Lila sharply ordered. "We'll work fast and scratch away as much gold as we can out from under here before darkness falls."

"All right, as long as that boulder overhead doesn't fall, too," Ned said, looking unsure. "But I'd really hoped that we'd find a gold mine with gold nuggets sticking out of the walls as easy to pick as grapes off the vine."

"Me, too," Lila said, "but we'll take what we can get and be grateful for that. Now hurry off and get those rock picks!"

Ned left and Lila used her pocketknife as she began to poke and dig at the gold. Ned didn't realize it, but if the boulder overhead didn't fall and crush them, they might be able to extract hundreds of dollars' worth of gold every day they could stand the risk of being crushed under tons of rock.

She worked fast and furiously with her pocketknife as the light quickly faded. Lila was about ready to see what was taking Ned so long when she heard a gunshot, then another and another.

"Oh my gawd!" she whispered, shoving her just-extracted pebbles of gold in her pants and rushing out from under the boulder to see what was going on.

Had the grizzly sow suddenly appeared and attacked Ned?

No, she thought, it was probably far worse than that!

"It's that banker from Grants and three others!" Ned cried, almost knocking Lila down as he scrambled back under the towering boulder where they'd just found Bixby's lost gold. "I was almost to the horses when they came into sight. They saw me first and opened fire!"

"John Jacob is way up here?"

"That's right. And three others. Lila, they didn't wait a heartbeat but just opened fire!"

"They know the gold is up here and they mean to have it all for themselves," Lila said. "And now we're trapped at the head of this canyon without horses. Dammit, Ned, I left my rifle in its scabbard, never thinking that we'd need it way up here!"

"What are we going to do?"

Lila thought about that a moment and then she drew her pistol from her holster. "They've got us boxed in against this cliff and the only good news is that they can't outflank us."

"But they'll have our horses. Our food. We've got nothing here."

"We've still got our lives, Ned. And after dark falls, we've got to figure a way to climb out of this canyon, fight through the deep snow up on the summit, and get the hell off Skull Mountain!"

"But you know the banker. He must be a reasonable man. Maybe you can talk him into letting us go away for equal shares of the gold we can get off this boulder we're under."

"Don't be a fool," Lila said harshly. "John Jacob doesn't share *anything*."

A bullet ricocheted off the huge boulder overhead. "They're moving in on us, Ned. Let's make a stand and hope that it gets dark real fast; otherwise our bones will soon join those four skeletons."

Chapter 19

Longarm and Homer Monroe had ridden their horses almost to death. After leaving the KC Ranch, they'd kept pushing well after dark and were thankful that the moon was almost full, clearly revealing the tracks of the four men they had been desperately attempting to overtake.

"Custis, how on earth can we keep this pace up?" Homer Monroe asked. "My horse is almost finished."

"I know," Longarm said, studying the rising moon. "But we're well up the mountain, and damned if I didn't hear gunshots a second or two ago."

"Gunshots?"

"That's right. Didn't sound like thunder to me. Don't talk anymore, Homer. Let's just push on toward the summit. We ought to be near the top of this mountain before daybreak."

"I don't know if my horse can make it that far without rest."

Longarm's reply was flat and uncompromising.

"Then hang back and rest your horse, because I'm gonna keep pushing on."

"I'll stick with you, by gawd!"

"Do the best that you can, Homer. I didn't ask you to come along and I won't ask you to kill that fine horse."

"If it comes down to my horse or the life of Miss Chandler, I'll ride until my horse drops dead."

"Me, too," Longarm said, forcing the palomino to its limits.

Several hours later they found a campsite not long abandoned. Longarm's eyes followed the trail that turned toward a dark canyon. "How are you and your horse doing, Homer?"

"I'm saddle galled and my horse is so tired he's constantly stumbling."

"Rest him and yourself," Longarm urged the hotelman. "I'll keep riding. I think the shots I heard came from near the top of that canyon."

"I'm going to get down and walk my horse for a while."

"Do that," Longarm said. "Maybe I'll do the same. But we have to keep moving."

"I know. I know."

They walked their horses up the trail and there was never a doubt in Longarm's mind that they were following the four men and that the four men were following Lila and Ned up Skull Mountain. Just before daybreak, they heard more shooting and it was close now. Real close.

"Homer, can you go any farther?"

"I didn't think I could," came the weak reply. "But hearing those gunshots just now made me think otherwise."

"Let's tie our horses off this trail and go ahead on foot. Make sure that you have your rifle ready."

"I will. Believe me, I will."

Longarm and the hotelman left their horses and started climbing. They were dead tired and the air was so thin that they had to stop often and rest just long enough to catch their wind and refill their tortured lungs. But as the sun arose over the peaks, they heard more shooting and it was very close now.

"Stay low and quiet," Longarm ordered as he hurried forward with a rifle in his fists. *"Real quiet."*

Suddenly, they were upon the four men, just shadows in the rapidly growing light. "Jacob!" Longarm shouted. "It's United States Marshal Custis Long. All of you, drop your weapons!"

The one that Longarm recognized as Henry Brody had no intention of surrendering to face a certain hangman's rope. He spun on his heels, drawing his six-gun, but the rock and loose footing caused him to lose his balance and fire wide. Longarm took aim and drilled Brody through the heart and then heard Homer Monroe's rifle booming close behind him as they both fired on the men desperately scrambling for cover.

Banker John Jacob was the only one to reach the rocks, but only moments later, two shots rang out from above and then there was nothing but echoes passing into silence.

"Lila!" Longarm shouted. "It's Custis! I've got Homer Monroe here with me! Are you and Ned all right?"

"Yes!" she cried, suddenly jumping up as if from the earth to stand silhouetted against the sunrise. "We're still alive!"

Minutes later they found John Jacob lying where he'd fallen deep into a crevice between huge rocks. Longarm, Ned, Lila, and Homer stood above the man and watched him fight for the last few moments of his life.

"Who were the four men we found executed at the mine?" Lila called down to Jacob. "Who were they?"

The rich banker looked up at her and managed a bitter smile. When he spoke, blood frothed from his lips and stained his expensive white silk shirt. "You'll never know, my dear woman. And you'll never find that . . . that gold."

"John, we *did* find it!"

His smile turned into a snarl as he gazed up at them with hatred. "You're . . . you're lying!"

Lila reached into her pocket and then spread the gold she'd just found across the palm of her hand. "I'm not lying to you. Look! Pure gold nuggets. Small, but there are a lot more where these came from, not twenty feet from where I'm standing."

His eyes bugged and he managed to raise a hand upward toward them. "Where . . . ?"

Lila dropped a tiny nugget down to land on the dying man's bloody chest. "John, you had Henry Brody murder my parents. Isn't that the way it was?"

"Your parents were gawdamn *old*. Henry Brody wanted to do the job in revenge for what your father did to his family. He would have murdered Kenyon for nothing!"

"Brody is dead and already on his way to hell," Longarm shouted down to the man gasping and choking for his last breath. "And judging from what I'm seeing right now, so are *you*."

He pulled his eyes away from the dying man and turned to Lila and Ned. "Are we gonna be rich?"

"Not quite," she told him, "but judging from the vein of gold we just found, none of us, including Homer, will ever have to worry about money again."

Longarm gave her a big, happy smile. "That's plenty good enough for me."

"Me, too," Ned told them, his eyes watching as Jacob coughed blood and died down in the deep crevice. "Does anyone want to go spend some time traveling in Europe?"

"Not me," Longarm said without a moment's hesitation. "I've still got a badge and job as a federal lawman."

Lila held Longarm's eyes for a long moment before she turned to Ned Corey. "I might want to go with you to Europe. Do you still intend to be a cattle rancher?"

"I definitely do."

"That's real good to hear, Ned."

And with those few words from her mouth, Longarm realized he would soon be heading back to Denver alone . . . but as a far wealthier man.

Watch for

LONGARM AND THE INNOCENT MAN

the 376th novel in the exciting LONGARM
series from Jove

Coming in March!

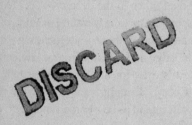